OPEN CUT

OPEN CUT

J. M. O'Neill

HEINEMANN: LONDON

William Heinemann Ltd
10 Upper Grosvenor Street, London WIX 9PA
LONDON MELBOURNE TORONTO
JOHANNESBURG AUCKLAND

First published 1986
Copyright J. M. O'Neill 1986
SBN 434 55339 5

Printed and bound in Great Britain by
Billing and Sons Ltd,
Worcester

From the property in Highgate, on a quiet road now, one could look out across a great obtuse segment of London, in the middle distance pick a spire or a dome: Shoreditch, St Paul's, a high-rise bank, the Telecom needle. Closer, at the foothills, there was perhaps only the red-brick turrets of St Pancras Station with its head above bilge water. But Mercer House – 'Mercer' was Nally's doing – had been a substantial dwelling surrounded by woods and green fields when wrought-iron rails and loco-motives were still on drawing-boards, and horses of flesh and blood daily made the unremarkable trip from Stockton to Darlington.

It was still detached now, and a few trees remained, stately but manicured; borders of shrubs too. It sat on a generous half-acre of marble-flecked asphalt, surveying the inexorable scab of London, tidemarks of grime coming and going down a little further at Archway and its environs. The closeness of seam and squalor somehow enhanced its dignity and that of its mere centenarian neighbours.

Nally treated it with loving care, respect. From a distant East Anglian dockyard he had salvaged staunch Victorian bollards and chains to fence off his forecourt between entrances and leave unimpeded an aspect of such permanence and har-mony. On a small unobtrusive plinth a cast-bronze plate said 'Mercer House'. When asked, he liked to explain that of course Whittington had been an opulent mercer, togger-out of the elite and with a couple of royal trousseaux to his credit. And it was an opportunity to explain the cat mythology, too, with a sting in the tail: Whittington had dabbled in coal, you see, and coal-schooners had been 'cats'. But of course 'Cat House' ... well!

In the bitterly cold stillness of early morning a light or two shone in the ground floor: cleaners on the move. It had a complement of thirty guests, discreet transient persons spending not overlong periods at embassies or hospitals or lecture-rounds or the like; and always the money up front. Bed and breakfast and a residents' bar at evening time. Nally didn't want people who couldn't afford to eat out. Their cars were parked back and front now, black-frosted to dullness and opacity.

Nally's quarters, as he liked to call them, were at its most remote corner. An original oak door, a single piece, and around it lintel and jambs adzed and immovable. The hinges and lock were modern and very special. There was a study, a bedroom, a luxurious bathroom, all with low-beamed ceilings. The bedroom and bathroom had small embrasured windows with folding shutters that were opened and barred at night-time. A little fortress.

At six o'clock Nally was awake. Waking was like cleverly stealing up on consciousness and taking it by surprise without a movement or a murmur. There was a certain trick about it. Motionless, he opened his eyes in the darkness and waited for thoughts to take shape, relished the warmth, the softness of his bed as if deliberately to sharpen the hardship of leaving it. But waking at six was a comfort or Nally would have slept until midday; he liked only very occasionally to walk to the fringes of his luxury and peer beyond the wall at austerity. To peer was sufficient.

'Phone calls 1–2–3', he had written on a scrap-pad: he dialled McLeod.

'Nothing unusual?'

'Nothing.'

Nally's voice was a comforting handshake, not easily placed, London certainly, but carefully honed: spontaneity might be something he had rehearsed and perfected over the years, and he could laugh very pleasantly.

2

There is a London frame – Bow Bells London – not tall, stocky, a shade overweight and the face, with good crowded teeth, fleshy too. Nally was like that: carefully darkened hair to let the grey shine through a little; a smart dresser. He was fifty, had come through the seventh climacteric unscathed, as he liked to put it.

'Our man is on a dummy run this morning,' he told McLeod. 'The driver, you know?'

'He's up to it, isn't he?'

'Oh yes.' Nally thought about Hennessy for a moment. 'Quite good. Very useful. Unusual, in fact.'

'A lot of rehearsals, isn't it?'

'Only two.'

McLeod made harsh border or Tyneside sounds that could be called regional and were found somehow 'charming' or 'endangered' by plummy-voiced old puff-balls on the afternoon remnants of steamtime radio. It was more the growl of a street-fighter but he was a mild light-boned man, tall, forty perhaps – astute, was Nally's assessment, but lazy – and a collector of what he found odd or beautiful and could afford. Because he looked neither special nor a policeman he was a special policeman. Nally considered it. Special people were like that, with a shrug giving costume the crease and hang of an everyday rag: unremarkable. And little contractors were hardly special or reputedly cerebral, that was certain. But Nally was. He knew it. Hennessy? A truck driver? Unlikely, yes. But he was: slightly special, of course, that was the trick.

'Only two?' McLeod said. 'I thought it was more.'

'Just two,' Nally confirmed. 'This morning is dress rehearsal, without dress, you could say. Next week is performance.'

'Unusual, the driver, you said?'

'Ideal for the occasion.' Nally left a long silence. 'But too good, perhaps. You understand?'

'Over-qualified?'

'That's it. A pity. I've used him a couple of years now. Small trips no bother. But when it's big there's bait. Next week, when the curtain's down, we'll have a tidy up, I think.'

'Whatever you say.'

3

'I have a site at Walworth now,' Nally said with a sudden shift of humour. 'Deep sewers. A lot of old jars rooted up with the spoil. "Cherry toothpaste patronised by the Queen for beautifying and preserving teeth and gums." All that kind of rubbish. Bottles too with marbles in the necks.'

'Interesting,' McLeod was saying.

'And a paperweight, I think, glass, perfect, all red flowers. Very nice. B1848 on the back, if that means anything?'

'Bacarrat,' McLeod said.

Nally smiled, he could feel McLeod's excitement. 'We'll have lunch one day soon. I'll bring everything.'

'Fine.'

Down at Highbury McLeod's phone was at his bedside; he liked his morning sleep.

'Our little mutual "archivist", Cleary?' Nally said. 'Well, is he?'

'Oh yes.'

Phone calls like this were routine and yet without pattern, a sudden opening and shutting of doors so that after a scattering of words an image remained. And there were afternoon and evening calls too: random and haphazard visitations of Nally, so that he was never unexpected.

His study had the matt silence of a cork floor, beautifully made with brown and burnt yellows and at peace with ancient oak. His desk, plain chairs, a table with marquetry, a sea chest, were all fine; and even the open gasfire and its surround found a place. The house was centrally heated but Nally's quarters were exempted. He preferred cool moist air; and dummy logs and naked flame, however contrived, when it was time for sloth.

The walls, hardly more than seven feet high, were panelled with deep cream plaster, unadorned except for a great mounted street map of London to its extremities. And in the corner by Nally's desk old blown-up snapshots were hung: parents, almost ludicrously young, and a virile grandparent outside their Stepney beer-house, holding him aloft like a missile. There was a date and the legend, 'The Day the War Broke Out'. Nally didn't remember it: he had been four. At six he had been successively orphaned, abandoned, cherished. The young face

4

hadn't made it back from the Beaches and the blonde cheeky schoolgirl beside him had gone off with a soldier, a Yankee soldier.

But the old man, suddenly young, had held the fort with sweat and roguery and a great succession of birds and dolly-mops, most of them screwed and unpaid when they left; and he had remained the indestructible Celt, clever and perverse as he had been in the last Edwardian days when he had arrived. The other pictures were of Nally, the student, the athlete, the scrapper in fighting crouch with his trophies; Nally, short-back-and-sided for a two-year stint of soldiering when he had learned a whole new bag of tricks.

He was smiling now. There was a knock on the door and he called out, 'Yes, Helena.' She had a key.

Helena shone with austerity: inornate, flattering clothes, an almost saintly tight-skinned face; the merest trace of accent: Austrian perhaps. She put a cup of tea and a plate with a single oatmeal biscuit on his desk.

'There's frost this morning,' she said.

'Yes, Helena.'

'You should light that gasfire, have a little heat in the room.'

'No, Helena.'

She went off, laughing softly, as if his reply, changeless, unvarying, had reached a saturation point where humour touched it . . .

Phone call 2: he dialled Feehan's number at Paddington and it was answered before the first jangle could explode.

'Good morning,' Feehan said.

An arrogant voice, Nally heard: just enough deference. Feehan was a gaffer – agent, Feehan would prefer – with the company's prestigious perk, a Merc, silver-grey, second-hand of course. Nally didn't push showroom models at hatchet-men, thick micks out of costume in shirts, ties and business suits. Feehan's hat, too, to hide creeping baldness before his twenties were out, was an offence: pearl-grey, indigo-banded, an un-fortunate choice meant for more delicate flamboyancy than building-sites could offer.

'Good morning,' Nally said easily. 'Any problems?'

5

That kind of admission could only be terminal. Feehan was a scourge, a bull-whip, a sledge-hammer, a hirer, a firer; mobocracy must smoulder about him, only smoulder, a delicate balance. Conflagration, and with it he perished.

Nally was looking towards his street map, at Walworth in fact, but his innocuous questions ranged across other sites and battle-grounds, hither, thither, almost haphazardly, so that he arrived quietly at his destination without finality or a change of pitch.

'How's Walworth?'

'Bad ground.'

'The heading, the tunnel? Who's in the tunnel?'

'Kirwan.'

'Past it a bit, isn't he?'

'Almost.'

'Progress?'

'If he's watched.'

'Stay on site a few days. Poke around, you know? Prod, prod, prod!' Nally seemed suddenly to remember spoil, but for Feehan he called it, 'Muck?'

'Fair amount.'

'Who's on it? Who's on muck?'

'Hennessy.'

'Good, is he? Good driver, you think?'

Feehan paused; Nally was pleased at the disparagement, the needle. 'He gets by,' Feehan said eventually. 'Clever bastard, you understand, sees everything, sees nothing.'

'Give him the odd prod. Prod everyone.' Nally looked at his watch: seven fifteen. 'I won't keep you,' he said.

Feehan's flat at Paddington was another perk in fact: an incitement, a grease, a push towards addiction, Nally sometimes joked. Feehan's greed was tight as a trap, and luxury – mere comfort and second-time round possessions in Feehan's case – powerful as poppy seed. But Nally made the price: beads of sweat and blood the only wampum.

Feehan was vain too. Greater violence than his own, violence beyond his range, that stunned and horrified, the deafening terror of torn limbs, spears of glass and wood, bodies skinned

6

and limp as jelly, filled him with breathless fear and wonder. And terror, open-handed, gratuitously given! He was drawn to the fringes of a dark world, merely to peer, rub shoulders, pass time of day; to the fringes, too, where it cost him nothing: a drink perhaps, a bed now and then for the shadows, the journeymen Jacobins on such deadly itineraries. Their proximity was like shrill unattainable desire.

And fortuitous, Nally thought, that Feehan at Paddington had become a beacon for McLeod and Cleary who lay in wait to log arrivals and departures of an endangering species; and send out unhindered the 'ringed' journeymen once more to lay flare paths to friend and foe.

Nally was pleased with it all.

Feehan would drive to King's Cross now where Nally's trucks were marshalled, and the shrouded amorphous labour force climbing aboard. He might hire a few, fire a few, let his rancour rain on them all. By seven thirty there would be an empty street, the diesels hammering out to scars in suburban avenues, stripped roadways, cranes bent over gaping manholes, broken concrete skin and sour muck, for a week or a month or forever. And on and on.

Nally sipped the dark brown almost milkless tea Helena had brought him. He had reached judgment on Hennessy and was glad of it: next week would be the final run for Hennessy; decision had hovered for a long time and finally roosted. There was always an aftermath of agreeable fulfilment when problems, irksome rather that insurmountable, had been resolved. But somehow the glow was less warm in contemplation of Hennessy's 'demise'. Hennessy was good. There was a sense of waste. Still, he had decided . . .

At seven thirty he made the remaining call. In reverie he had forgotten his tea and a broken metallic skin had settled on it. He pushed it aside.

He dialled Bredin's number at the Repair Yard in Haringey. He could afford to be less guarded with Bredin, all twenty tobacco-smelling stone of him. Bredin was hard, blunt, changeless, honest. You could take him or leave him.

'How do I find you this morning?' Nally asked.

7

'A day older,' Bredin said.

Nally laughed. 'A lot of casualties in?'

'Take your pick,' Bredin said. 'Fucked-up pumps, hammers, steels, compressors, mixers, dumpers, third-rate mechanics?' Bredin's words had a coarse emery resonance. 'A beer-sick blacksmith coughing and puking down there in the smoke? And up my arse . . . hear it? . . . that's another phone on the boil with some ape at the end of it!'

'I can hear it,' Nally said. 'Doesn't Cleary answer phones?'

'He's a clerk. He comes at nine,' Bredin said.

'Ah yes. I won't waste your time. I'll drop in one morning.'

'Do that.'

Nally was pleased at the bluntness: reassuring. It was moving on towards eight. In a few minutes he would walk out in the air that was still below freezing and on his hilltop pathway peer out from among the trees and shrubs across London to its most distant skyline. A light breakfast then before the day's importunities snatched him off . . .

Seventy, eighty thousand, McLeod reckoned. Nally considered it. Time would tell: another week. In seven days it would be no dummy run for Hennessy: the real thing, the big one, Hennessy might call it. He hoped Hennessy was big enough too.

There was no anxiety for himself, of course: he, McLeod, old friends, old hands were out of reach. But Hennessy? Hennessy failed was Hennessy adrift, man on the run. He knew the rules. And in the turbulence of troughs and changing times, jack-the-lads, desperadoes, armed bandits, must expect savage swingeing strokes of justice. A blunder, twenty years, Nally reckoned. With even the faintest ring of paddy-provenance twenty years would scarcely be a breeze-ripple on an oily courtroom.

And why not! When the need arose in Nally's world his 'justice' too was swift and final.

Hennessy, an each-way loser. A pity of course. A casualty, nothing more, his days numbered. But it was strange to wish him spared from one justice for the jaws of another.

In contemplation of failure Nally was only appalled, saddened at the real enormity of loss: seventy, eighty thousand was a lot of money. McLeod's gathered whispered intelligences, Nally's expertise, all at one moment wagered on the skill of Hennessy who might 'get the trip' or bungle it . . .

Nally paused in his walking, looked down over three miles of city towards Highbury where McLeod had his not insubstantial roots – a solid property, a more than modest investment – and gave cheap bed and board to Cleary. It worked well, a successful graft, McLeod agreed. Nally had arranged it of course.

A mile or so north, and a shade eastwards, down somewhere in the awful frozen streets, in a sea of rimed slate and chimney pricks, pinheads in the distance, was the Repair Yard and Bredin in the morning grind and stridence of phone bells. About nine, ten, certainly before lunch – Nally always counted foibles – Cleary would move from McLeod to Bredin: he was a nark and a clerk. Nark and clerk: the jingle, the assonance, had occurred to Nally at the time. He had arranged it of course. Cleary narked for McLeod, clerked for Bredin.

Down below in a few square miles of rooftop tundra that were Nally's foothills a day was beginning. From King's Cross the trucks had speared out long since to the coloured pins on Nally's map and, at Walworth, Feehan, the gaffer, the unskilled, the headman, was walking the ground.

The pathway beneath Nally's feet was rock-hard, frost-cracks here and there, and late leaves grey as mud lay curled in lifelessness; black limbs and digits of trees were desolate against the icy sky. Nally climbed the pavements and passed the elegance of fine detached town-houses of single doorbells, tended gravel drives, shrubberies, attendant garages. In five minutes he was crossing the forecourt of his hotel, seeing always the fine cut-stone, tall foppish chimneys, all the loving embellishment that artisans had bestowed; and inside, the inherited peace, something intrinsic, that Nally had been careful not to disturb. He looked: it was reserved and sober in the pale blue morning. When he reached the warmth and calm of the foyer Helena, passing, said, 'Good morning, Mr Nally.'

He took a newspaper from Reception and at his dining-room table unfolded its broadsheet, glanced across the grey conservatism of its priorities: it was a world of mayhem, cataclysmic, dog-eat-dog but a daily comfort to Nally in almost blessed obscurity. Nally made his own rules. Less complicated.

A four-line snippet at the foot of the page said, 'London Bomb Scare'. For a day or two McLeod and his counterparts would be treading softly . . .

Seventy, eighty thousand. Nally thought again of Hennessy now on the Hertfordshire roads, a dummy run: behind the flintiness, the unexpected warmth in Hennessy's face at close quarters, a kind of sobriety; hard too, and thirty was a hungry age to look out at the nothingness of early mornings. Clever, sees everything, sees nothing, Feehan said.

Good, Nally was thinking.

After six o'clock, further down the slopes from Nally's first stirrings, at Archway, another seamy foothill still blessed with darkness, Kirwan crept up the stairs of a boarding house from Maisie's bedsitter. He was wearing a vest and underpants and carried his clothes in an untidy bundle before him.

When he had reached the top landing, tiptoeing towards security, the door of Hennessy's room was opened and Hennessy said very softly, 'Come on in a minute.'

Kirwan groped his way across the landing. 'What the Christ are you up to?' he said. 'You don't have to move this early with a load up.' He got into Hennessy's bed and covered himself. 'When are the shoots open? You could be flat on your back for an hour yet.' He closed his eyes and exhaled the weariness of love-making.

There was no light, only the darkness had lessened and the bare walls of the room were faintly visible; it was the hushed beginning of workaday before urge and movement pushed thoughts into hiding; you could see the sky, Hennessy thought, and almost hear the wind blowing along it. In the gloom he watched the comfortable shape of Kirwan beneath the clothes and waited: Kirwan would be remembering the comfort of Maisie or wondering in drowsiness if ever there might be a magic morning when Maisie and he would get up late and smoke a fag as they walked down together to the pub at midday opening. That was the life.

He put his hand on Kirwan's shoulder and shook him, put a cigarette in his mouth. 'I won't be on site until late. Twelve, later maybe. I don't know. I want you to fix it.'

Kirwan might have nodded.

'Do you hear?'

'For Christ's sake!' Kirwan scowled at him through the half-light; his body ached at the bleak onset of another day. 'You're broke down, you're broke down,' he said with a kind of unquiet resignation. 'I saw you under the bonnet when I left. Will that do?'

'Fine,' Hennessy appeased him. 'An air-lock. Tell Feehan at King's Cross: Hennessy's air-locked with a load up, he'll be late in Walworth. That's all.'

'That brainless goat couldn't tell an air-lock from his arsehole.'

Hennessy bent close to him. 'Tell him what I said,' he warned. 'No more, OK?'

He stood at the window. A milk-float droned into the greyness, rattled its cargo at every bump. A few yawning lights showed from the forlorn towers of a high-rise outcrop.

Kirwan was motionless, supine: grey matted hair, a blur of face, the unlighted cigarette hanging askew from his lips. After a little while he said, 'You're rustling for Nob Nally again this morning . . . I can smell it. You're fucking mad . . .'

'Don't upset Feehan,' Hennessy cut across him. 'Say I had a breakdown. No more.'

For a moment Kirwan's grip on anxiety and impatience faltered. 'Bollicks to you!' he said, jabbing out words in darkness. 'And Feehan! That poisonous poxed-up goat!' His anger melted away but disquiet, maybe foreboding, hovered. 'And watch your step.'

Hennessy was silent.

'Watch your step. That's a Hard Man on the Hill when the humour takes him.' The acid in the raw of Kirwan's stomach gathered and erected in a deep keening lament. 'You're only the lad, the runner, you know? What is it? Fags, booze? And what do you get! We should have upped sticks and gone a long time ago . . . a long time ago . . .'

'This morning is for *me*,' Hennessy said eventually. 'A little trip. Everything should be dull and quiet, understand?'

'For you?'

'That's right.'

Kirwan sat up in bed, hunched his shoulders against the cold: he saw that Hennessy wore a dark blazer jacket, pale cords, a roll-neck sweater. Kirwan's ageing face sagged below a grey tangled fringe of hair. 'What's up, for Christ's sake!'

Hennessy was pulling on dirty muck-stained trousers to cover the elegance; and then rubber boots, a donkey jacket, a cap. In a sports hold-all he put shoes, a woollen black and white striped scarf, a mackintosh.

The clothing confused Kirwan. Watching the packing, the dissemblance, he said, 'Snatching crates of fags and booze is a villain's game. Nally's game. In a front door, out the back. You need doors. Nally has doors. Pubs, clubs, a house on the Hill . . .'

'I know,' Hennessy said.

Kirwan lit the cigarette and his bleakness flared for a moment. 'But you'd have thought of that, wouldn't you?' he said.

'Yes.'

Kirwan was on the danger side of forty-five, nearing the fag-end: the limbo of doss and Giroland opened its gates for him.

'This one is *cash*,' Hennessy said.

'Cash?'

'You could call it promotion, I suppose.' There was no humour in his voice.

'Cash? One man?'

'That's right'

'You're out of your mind,' Kirwan said at the end of a long silence. 'Not Nally. No one takes that animal. He'd set you up like a road sign. You'd be an old man if ever you saw Camden Town again. But that's your business.'

'It is,' Hennessy said; he tightened up and prepared to leave.

Kirwan saw the gun, neat and tidy, at his waist. 'Jesus!' he said.

'I couldn't stand another fifteen winters, could you? You'll be over the hill from sixty, or gone to Leytonstone. And me?' Hennessy looked hard at him. 'Grey thatch and a belly hanging, like that.'

The closeness of pain and fading power lingered a moment.

'Sixty,' Hennessy said again.

'I know.'

'Soft pedal with Feehan, with everyone.'

Kirwan nodded, was silent until Hennessy moved.

'Fags?'

'On the table.'

'Take care . . .' he started, but Hennessy had gone.

He took the cigarettes and went next door to his room. Even in the distance he heard the roar of Hennessy's truck as it pulled away and faded. His own agonising hours ahead in a four-by-three glimmer of tunnel and then the staggering sweetness of Maisie's perfume assailed him in turn, and he sat in darkness, gathering himself.

Suddenly time had flown and he began to dress hurriedly, impatient and wild with tangled clothes he could hardly remember pulling off, and thought of Maisie and what a fine bird she was. No, not a bird, he faulted himself: a fine woman. He felt again the excitement of Maisie clinging to him. He should marry her, he pondered; or ask her, anyway. But then it might be a mess: if there weren't trips down the empty stairs and the awful suspense of tapping at her door it might be dull as a drain.

Remembering the warmth of her body, how gently she looked at him, kissed his face and shoulders, brought an overwhelming flood of tenderness. She was a fine woman. At the mirror he rubbed his ageing skin, studied the irreparable damage of years. He was lucky to have a bird like Maisie. What did she see in him? Christ, if he told Hennessy he might marry her . . .

Envisaging it, there was an urge to shout aloud in his flight to the bus stop but sobriety held him like a clamp and it occurred to him that he might never see Hennessy again.

He tightened his coat about him, almost ceased to think, wished he stood at the end, not the beginning, of a day.

*

Hennessy bought cigarettes at a we-never-close Pakistani shop near Archway, in a street that had given up its gates and iron railings in some war effort and victory hadn't been honourable enough to put them back; perhaps the rot had begun then and now there was decrepitude everywhere. The Iron Duke's Tavern, tarted in blue and red and orange, traded in Happy Hours, Sunday Strip, Monday Topless, Tuesday Rock, Wednesday Doubles . . .

Hennessy scanned the long converging pavements. A few drops of frosty rain fell and the cold air moved a little. He bent low beneath the body of the truck and found the speedo-cable. He tugged at it until it snapped. Then he climbed into the cab of the truck. In the driving-mirror he could see dustbins towering above eroded brick walls, naked and discarded as the Iron Duke strippers, and an old man with a hand-cart was scavenging.

He found himself watching everything with the fierce shallow interest of someone escaping a thought; he wanted the chill of expediency to grip him again, push him on his way, but momentarily the trick of it was lost; he could only reach out for embitterment. The old man groped in the dustbins without ever seeming to find anything and moved out of sight, and greyness was barely seeping down between the brick houses.

He thought again of Nally, to fix him clearly and unfavourably in his mind, but it was like boasting a terrible injury, searching for tiny scars. You did Nally's bidding, muck or marauding, and he paid on the nail. Straight up, that was something. There were blurred but still discernible codes for Hennessy; little shredded moments of honesty surfaced and were sour with discomfort. The dupery, the rip-off sat heavily. Thieving was easy, it needed anger, hardness, that was all. But the double-deal was something else. He drove through the rolling fringes of Hornsey and Crouch End that were hardly awake and down towards the Greek world of Haringey and Turnpike; as he swung from Crouch End he caught for a moment a glimpse of Highgate Wood like a distant frosted Olympus. Was Nally sleeping or waking? How many pieces of himself had Nally traded to climb so high? Did everyone trade? Nally, glossed, stove-baked, he thought suddenly, would sniff at morality like wet paint.

Hennessy knew the House at Highgate, the pubs, a few of them, the clubs, some little part of Nally's estate, he supposed. The House might be sacrosanct, he had never been called there. But once in winter darkness he had stood, uninvited, on the forecourt and knew at once the outlandish distance to be travelled.

When there was humping work on the slate, Nally liked to talk things over with a drink and pub noises about him. Very friendly.

'I was born in this house,' he had said to Hennessy once. 'Iron fireplace, sawdust floor, counter just there, oak barrels, brass taps, high up behind it. Took a bit of hoisting. Gut-twisters. Now look at it . . .'

Carpeted, warm, lighted with care, its furniture right, everything right . . .

He had met Nally a few times since – always a different pub, a drink, a kind of effortless conversation of humour and reminiscence, and the information fed in at spaces along the way.

Only weeks ago since Nally had said, 'This one is different, another game, another board, different pieces. Dummy runs. Cover the ground a couple of times, maybe more. Know it so you don't think anymore. Understand? . . .'

'Yes.'

'Now, how can I put it?' Nally seeming to search about for words that have already been carefully gathered and weighed. 'Take the fight game: he comes the hard way, does the homework, goes the distance. See, get it?'

'Yes.'

'But . . .' Nally considering again. 'Push him in too soon? He's knocked? Why? Not ready, see?'

'Yes.'

'Not ready . . . Now this little shop I have in mind won't be ready either. Our little shop is a little bank but pushed in too soon. You'll see. That's the time to move . . .'

'Yes.'

'You'll have a good pay day.'

In the diesel winter of the cab Hennessy felt the scorch of

loneliness, even fear, and beyond the faint last stirrings of blamelessness there arrived the deeper shadow of treachery. Spleen for Nally should burn, he knew, but it was a poor inadequate spark; indifference, thick-skinned, if he could give it space, was the thing. Indifference was callus, arrogance, cold enthusiasm. He tried to think of Nally gathering fairytale plans, loving them, storing them like precious ornaments in his mind, but Nally always emerged from his corner, chin in shoulder, hands high, ready for the strike . . .

It was a quarter before seven, the street lights burning, night-time still in suburban bedrooms with clocks on bedside tables moving on in the darkness towards the clamour of waking time. He drove the truck deep into the red-brick warrens, leaving black virgin tracks in the rime. Down, beyond, was the iron scar of a railway bridge; and nearer, behind its walls and gates, the huge scattered blocks of the old Fever Hospital. The diesel engine whined on the gradients: fifteen tons of wet muck was a good load but he had twenty piled up behind him. He could feel the drag of it on the sudden humps of road; he saw his marker ahead: a blunted cul-de-sac, a caff, a phone booth, a surgical goods shop with a veterinary display of apparatus scattered on wallpapered shelves. A little beyond them he halted at the open gates of Bredin's Repair Yard. Except for a pilot-light at the entrance it was in darkness. He climbed down and shouted into the jungle of disembowelled vehicles and machinery.

A fitter came up out of the greasy pool of shadow. 'Yeah?' he said: a thick Midlands mumble it might be.

Hennessy nodded at the truck. 'The speedo cable is gone.'

'So what?'

'So I want a new one.'

'A couple of days, if you're lucky.'

'No speedo cable, no mileage for Bredin's logsheet,' Hennessy prodded him.

'You estimate it, professor. You know what that means?'

'As long as Bredin knows,' Hennessy said. 'Where is he?'

'He comes soon enough.'

'And Cleary?'

'Oh dear Christ!' The fitter spat and sucked his gums in

disparagement of Hennessy. 'Friend of yours is he, that dozy ponce? Might make it for nine or ten or eleven, lunchtime maybe. Have a seat.'

Hennessy took a long look at him. 'You won't forget to tell Bredin I reported it? The speedo cable.'

'I'll try to remember.'

'I wouldn't want a fiver chopped off my packet for not showing mileage.'

'Yeah ... yeah ... yeah ...'

On his way back to the truck Hennessy said, 'This is a shithouse. Forty-eight hours to fit a speedo cable. Christ help us!' He climbed into the cab.

The fitter bawled at him, 'You thick bastard! Know it all, don't you! One tool in a tool-box, paddy's magic wand! A pox of sites all round the town and showers of useless dossers like you on every one ... Piss off!'

Hennessy pressed the starter and blotted him out, turned back to the High Road. It had been important to upset the fitter: important, so that on Bredin's arrival he would go storming to the wooden office at the end of the yard. 'That clever half-cocked latch from Walworth was here!'

'Who?'

'Hennessy! Speedo cable! We should have teams on the hook, like fucking transplants! Bring him a cuppa while he squats on the bog! Speedo cable, he says!'

Bredin, huge and glaring, at his desk by the window.

'Yes?'

'You'd think he was running this kip.'

'Would you?'

'He needs a few spiky ones stuck up him.'

'I'll talk to him.'

A rumble of single syllables; but in a day or two when Cleary, thumbing through the sweated logsheets, called out his discovery, Bredin would nod and dismiss it and the door would be closed on Cleary's little searching mind.

Hennessy tightened his donkey about him, feeling the chill of cold air coming up from the floor of the cab. The road broadened out at the fringes of Tottenham and then narrowed again as if there might have been a village and perhaps a church a hundred years before the towering latticed jibs of football-floods and the ramparts of White Hart Lane.

Near Edmonton he saw a glimmer from an all-night filling station and pulled in across the empty forecourt that was still in construction: sand, ballast, trestles, discarded timber, shone with painted frost; two lighted pumps were extravagant in the darkness. The minder emerged, coughing, wheezing, trotted across the open space; beside him, jet black, a Dobermann glistened in health.

'Coming, coming,' he tried to articulate, but the breathless wheezing immobilised him; he rested across the bonnet of a wreck, waved to Hennessy for patience, indulgence.

'Jesus,' Hennessy whispered.

'Coming, coming!' he was in motion again, spat a great ball of gluey mucous on to a scrap heap and peered up at the cab.

'How many?' Like a gun, he pointed the nozzle at Hennessy. 'Personal service till the micro comes.'

Hennessy looked out beyond the chain of derelict houses: the sick cadaverous face disturbed him.

'Top-up?'

'Wait,' Hennessy said. 'Six. Six gallons. Cash.'

There was a flicker of awakening interest, the face tilted at him. 'Six, you said? Cash?'

'Yeah.'

'Shocking cold, isn't it?' he said, huddled in the lee of the pump. 'Feet as cold as the grave. With an oil stove,' he explained, 'the heat goes up. That's no bloody good to your feet unless you stand on your hands.' He had the lilting ding-dong tedium of Dublin quaysides or he might have scurried out from the Playhouse near the River, still with his tragi-comic face and costume and a pitful of gommy laughter in his ears. With each glance he assessed Hennessy. 'A Greek has this place,' he said. 'Greeks, very cagey people, you know. Kyriakides, he calls himself.'

The quirky steps, the grimace and squint, a body quickly growing old, the shape and colour of his face perhaps draining into an illness; the motionless Dobermann: Hennessy felt the

18

sharp image on his memory. He'd give him a pound for a drink.

'Cash,' Hennessy said. 'No receipt.'

It might have been a command. The little man stiffened to attention, mock-saluted; and then a glint of cock-a-hoop, of ineffable satisfaction came like the slow switch of a lamp. Close to Hennessy he said, 'I had you sussed coming in the gate. Odds on, a joker, early, on a private run, I told myself.' He laughed. An onslaught of breathlessness loomed and was defeated. 'Well, we must all make a flag when we can, eh?' He winked reassuringly to Hennessy. 'A lot of cash customers this morning. Bad times, you see? Everyone on the make.'

Hennessy nodded, compassion, solicitude faded, were thinning fast. He gave him a twenty and waited for change.

'Good luck,' he told Hennessy. 'There's an extra flag there. Have a jar yourself when the guv'nor's not looking.'

Hennessy nodded. 'You're better off than Kyriakides,' he told him; and, pulling away, he could see the indestructible wasted gnome lighting a dog-end, his shoulders twitching as he began to cough again.

Hennessy drove along the North Circular Road and at Colney Hatch Lane turned north again for Barnet; and the small tricksy figure, the little gull, gasped and choked in his mind for a moment. Nally wouldn't have been hoodwinked for an instant, he suddenly thought. Was there a splendid plan for little old wheezing tea-leaves stuck with the night-time stints and feet as cold as the grave?

'Old, Nally, counting the years, the rooms, the dying streets, all the flood tides missed.'

'You lose concentration at that kind of thing. He probably pisses it up and has nauseating affairs with filthy old rat-bags as wretched as himself.'

'His feet were cold. The heat from an oil stove, he said, goes up . . .'

'Did you tell him naked flame in a filling station is an offence?'

He had passed Whetstone Cross, moved down the smooth, undulating road over the last reaches of London. The morning

19

light caught the church tower on Barnet Hill, faded it a pale grey, lit the edges of roofs and chimneys on the High Street; in the distance, in the early quiet, it was old, magnificent, so unreal that it might have vanished when he reached it and there would only be a grassy hill and white roads stretching out to Potters Bar and Elstree and St Albans.

It was eight thirty. The cab had gathered an oily warmth but it was a winter's day beyond the thawed slush of the wind-screen: a vista of winter trees, tall dense broken ranks and the summer's lush crop lying in humus at their feet, patterns of frost like snail trails. And then suddenly the open sweep of tillage and grassland. He had pulled away from the main drags, moved into quieter lanes, followed Nally's pre-arranged roads, squandering time, matching time and place, until the last moments rushed him into action.

It was a village, a precise three miles ahead now, its church spire barely spiking into view. Left, on a radius, was Nally's target, once removed: a distant growing complex of brick and glass in construction, almost lost in a screen of afforestation. 'Environment, you know,' Nally had said, '. . . fenced off, a bit special, new, quiet, that kind of thing. But a lot of people you see, and our local bank man overloaded, out of puff . . . not ready, as we said.'

. . . The church spire was taller now, sharp-edged in the morning light and commuter traffic came and swept past in little clusters.

'I've covered the ground myself,' Nally explained. 'Yard by yard, a lot of times, a lot of weeks. A deal of work about you'll find; a lot of rubbish, untidy; cowboys, jobbers, cack-handed builders, painters, everywhere. And market-day of course. A square full of clapped-out bangers and push-carts. Greasy tippers don't raise an eyebrow . . .'

. . . Hennessy measured another mile, reached the first neat expensive little dwellings, hutches, detached and brooding on their appointed lots of grass and crazy paving. Little lands of nod and forgetfulness.

At a window a very tall man was silhouetted and Hennessy saw the room behind him was brilliantly red and comfortable:

Henderson, an ageing bank clerk with a distaste of market-days, was contemplating his diurnal march to the office. As if time had stood still, he peered out at the morning, seemed to grimace and recoil from it as he had precisely done a week before for Hennessy; and how many times for Nally?

Nally had plotted the morning walk from garden gate to bank door destination: a smile for Briggs, the hall porter, the stroking of shoes on the mat. Once he had almost counted the paces ...

'This Henderson?'

'Family man, picky, you know, slight limp, burn scars, ugly. Korea, I think.' Nally had painted him in quick brush dabs.

'If he baulks?'

'Clerks, duffs, also-ran johnnies, with school bills and mortgages, don't tend to be heroic.'

'All of them?'

'Conjecture is for weather experts.' Nally had smiled. 'Your problem. It's worth a thou' to come home safe. Foul it up, you're on your own. You understand, don't you?'

... Hennessy looked back at the window, red, like a Lautrec poster, Henderson a black shadow spilt across it: he would have come down to his red breakfast-room at the stroke of eight, very tall, frail; scar tissue dragging and paling at jaw and throat; and while a kettle heated, moments before an electric fire, salvaged pages of newspapers perused without interest. Market-day: the hovering thought of it unpleasant to him; staff early at their places; crowds like in a grocery store, a kind of shuffling noise in the office all day; and when it was over a smudged untidiness about everything, even the pavements and streets. Hennessy envisioned him for a moment, felt just an instant's compassion. For Henderson, days would have tangs: and market-days, sour, reminders of failure and ennui, that dignity in grubby confusion must seem to the onlooker funny, outrageous. Shirt-sleeves, tangled hair, schoolgirl cashiers: their world had crept in past him. He would have taken a cup of tea upstairs to his wife, reminded her of the time, that the children hadn't moved yet; and she would have shielded her eyes against the light.

'I might be a little late today, my dear.'

'Is somebody sick again?'

'No, it's market day.'

'Oh yes. Guy Fawkes tomorrow. Isn't it?'

' . . . certainly not before six.'

'Will you bring fireworks for the children?'

'Getting old for fireworks now?'

'Not too many. They're just a waste of money, really.'

'Yes.'

A knock on the children's doors before he went downstairs, a cup of tea standing by the window, contemplating the bright harsh day and the beleaguered enjoyment of walking to the office.

He might for a moment have glanced at the big laden tipping truck passing his gate, pushing against the flow of traffic as if carrying for his displeasure the accumulated filth of market-day into town.

After nine Hennessy saw him a little way off on the narrow village pavements. The truck was parked in the quiet fringes of the market; he had discarded the working clothes. The bank was hardly fifteen paces away, on the corner; morning workers went by, unnoticed, unnoticing. Hennessy watched him move down through the last moments of waiting, the streets growing busier about him, the old rakish air of hilly bottle-necks and chimneys awry in the frosty air, diminishing. Earlier, a friendly policeman had vanished to tea and toast and other custodian duties.

Henderson reached the traffic intersection, the rhythm, the timing near perfect. Hennessy watched him a moment and crossed to the other footway so that they moved, like acolytes converging on each other, to the bank door.

School children, shrieking in a battle of conversation, scurried between them.

Henderson, sentry-like, before the unobtrusive pencil of glass through which Briggs would inspect him, rang the door bell.

As the door opened Hennessy said, 'Oh, Henderson!'

The tall figure, gloves in hand, was beside him; a long rather ugly face and kind eyes, the pale shiny rawness of the burn scar giving him an extraordinary dignity; he had fought perhaps in more honourable and less skilful battles than the one he was so graciously entering.

'Ah, good morning,' he said by way of an almost apologetic inquiry: and careful to exclude not even the least of things, 'Good morning to you, Briggs.'

'Good morning, sir.'

An instant of smiling confusion; Hennessy pushed forward without effort and they were in the deserted hallway: the smell of floor polish, brass handrails, stillness. Hennessy leant back against the door and cut off the morning.

'Dear me,' Henderson said: he had felt no anxiety; he had liked the deep almost accentless voice of Hennessy, perhaps the slightest trace of north-country, Irish perhaps; educated of course; the macintosh was expensive; rugger man, make and shape of a good one, scarf, sports-case . . .

Hennessy held finger to lip for silence, brought the gun from inside his jacket.

This was the moment Nally pondered, when the actor might fail: a feeble movement, a false ring to a word, and the illusion would crumble . . .

Briggs, the porter, head down, lunged at him and he ripped open his scalp with a slash of the muzzle, left him clawing on the red polished floor.

'Get him on his feet,' he told Henderson quietly. 'And move.' He held open the glass door of the office and in a bizzare moment of Grand Guignol they were suddenly on stage.

From behind the counter masks of tragedy, fatuous in the moment of shock, gazed out as if from an ageing sepia of the past. Eight and a manager, Nally had said. He counted them. Henderson, exhausted, let the bloodied burden of the porter lie wounded at his feet.

Hennessy said, 'No alarms.' He held the gun at the pale leather of Henderson's neck.

A little girl, hardly out of school, sat at a telephone switch-board; she looked as if she might shriek with laughter at the madness of the morning. And then suddenly she was whimpering.

Hennessy aimed the gun at her; she gazed at him and the blood drained from her sickly face.

'Ring the manager's office,' he told her. 'Tell him Briggs has had a seizure.'

Henderson nodded, smiled reassurance and encouragement to her. 'Do as he says, there's a brave girl.'

It was a cramped unprepossessing room, still with a sloping desk or two, a wall map, insurance advertising, an old framed photograph of a stone building in the City; the coke fire was a fake but everything was old and beautifully preserved. Henderson's words might have been an airless tune hummed or whistled, a mannerism . . .

And then, as if by some magical transference of matter, the manager was instantly present: a dumpy weight-watching little fellow, somehow flash, from aviator's moustache to glittering shoes, perhaps fifteen years younger than Henderson. At the moment of alarm some tranquillising mechanism had cut in and he was glowingly pleasant, almost like Nally, Hennessy thought, unruffled by old recurring problems. He might have been about to say with gentle forbearance, 'Now chaps, what have we got here?', until Hennessy came slowly into focus, and the gun, and breathtakingly, the bleeding porter at Henderson's feet: a kind of exploding pietà.

'Everyone!' Hennessy said with a deliberate suddenness that set them in motion. 'Out here!'

A church clock somewhere close by was striking the quarter. They came out and faced him like frightened choristers. The manager's hands hung limply away from his body, twitched in a little spasm of rigor.

'Your office?'

He nodded.

'Get him in there,' Hennessy said: he pointed at the porter. 'Lift him. All of you.'

The manager's office was a heartless reproach to the tiresome longevity of the building, a stylistic adjunct, a place of avant-garde executive elegance: ceramics and shadowed walls, ceiling aglow, two Chagall prints and a tub of greenery; even time itself electrified behind a blank disc of stainless steel. And Briggs, the porter, awed by the status of his pall bearers, the blood from his head dripping unevenly on the carpet, was borne to his vault . . .

The numbered discs were turned, the bolts drawn, the inner cage surrendered. Henderson took the sports-case.

'Old money,' Hennessy said.

He watched them lay Briggs gently on the floor of the safe but, faithful servant ever, he struggled heroically to his feet in a token attempt to play the immemorial role of defending his betters.

Henderson stilled him. 'Don't overdo it, Briggsie, like a good fellow.'

It would have been nice to smile and reassure them, Hennessy thought for a moment: he nodded to Henderson, took from him the loaded sports-case, shut them in, pushed home the bolts, threw the light switch beside him, left them in darkness. It was nine twenty.

It took no more than ninety seconds to walk a leisurely hundred yards, Nally had estimated. Hennessy moved through the market untidiness, and beyond, to the quiet remoteness of parked vehicles. At nine thirty, in donkey and cap again, he had moved into the open country, pushing hard now. In an hour, perhaps a little longer, the early people, impatient ones, at the bank's closed doors, would whisper foul play and wonder.

At ten thirty he drew into a telephone box near Tottenham High Road. In the country lanes about Broxbourne he had changed, found a disused ballast pit to dump clothing and the frozen tons of muck and rubble from Walworth.

He telephoned Nally, stood and counted the ringing tones and knew that Nally too was counting them, prescribing for everyone certain spans of dignified waiting. In a few moments it was answered.

'Yes,' Nally said: immediate recognition. 'Everything in order then? No changes?'

'Just a little.'

'Details are your affair.'

'People did their pieces well . . . '

'Of course.' A trace of impatience in Nally's voice. 'Then next week for real. I needn't see you again. Ring me when you're clear. About this time. We can meet.'

'Wait,' Hennessy said.

'What is it?'

'A lot of money in my truck.' Hennessy looked out at the endless traffic of people and vehicles, waited in a long silence. 'We'll call it even-stephen, Nally. Down the middle. Everything went fine.'

'I see.'

'Your piece. Tonight. You know where I park. Help yourself. Lift the driving seat.'

'Where are you?'

'In town. Not running. I'll be in Walworth soon.'

Nally was laughing. 'You silly bastard,' he said, for a moment the steel glinting. 'You don't give me a fingers like that. You're in a lot of bother.'

'I'm expecting it.'

'I'll have to send someone to see you.'

'Tell him to expect a lot of bother too.'

He heard the snap of the receiver as Nally hung up: the first sounds of battle. In his room, down behind Archway, he counted the bundles – eighty-four thousand – and made his parcels. He buried his own under a mound of rotting clothes and boots in Kirwan's next-door doss: woodlice, even maggots, crawled in it. He put Nally's share under his driving seat and pushed for Walworth. It was turned the half hour, rising for twelve. Remembering Kirwan in his bed, the broken face, the fags, Maisie's perfume, it seemed that a whole endless day must have already passed.

Stroud Green was in a snarl of horn-locked buses, cars, minicabs, vans unloading; and he skirted it, crept into Green Lanes at Haringey Track. Greek Lanes now, he thought; Dalston and Kingsland were south and east of him and he would be aimed at London Bridge, and beyond it, Walworth.

Crossing the lights at Manor House, he glanced across and thought that in the distance he saw for a suspended moment of time, the pale face of Cleary, Bredin's clerk. An instant and he had passed; but the image remained with him and caution crept into his thoughts.

*

26

In the Repair Yard office there is another map of London tacked on the wall, unlike Nally's, a brown dust-embedded map. Cleary's table is against the wall and when he sits at it he is always facing the map and hardly ever sees it. Sometimes when he is pondering McLeod's shifty battlefields, the doorways, the long vigils, the attrition of patience and pride, anger and disquiet stir a little, the map jerks into perspective, the great roads leading out of the city grow darker, seem to move a little like the black dying legs of an insect and only the coloured pins of Nally's sites hold them in pain. Then he is pondering again and if the yard is still for a moment he can hear the clamour of traffic from the High Road.

Up there is movement and urgency; beyond it, behind the traffic and tailored shops, are ghettos of forgotten streets where people live in brick houses prescribed elegant to their rank when 'Good-Bye Dolly Gray' was the rage of the music-halls and tuppence on a horse-tram an hour's walk: the lace curtains are still there and china dogs on bamboo tables behind the windows; but often now cheap cafés man the entrances to the parking space of cul-de-sacs and crescents, and small teething industries squat like crabs wherever space offers; residents squabble with mechanics and truck drivers and send round-robins to the Borough Councils complaining of eye-sores and noise and foul language, and jump out of bed when the alarm clocks ring and rush off to work in dungarees and greasy caps. At seven thirty doors are opening and shutting everywhere and at eight hardly a soul stirring.

At midday it is almost a dead world.

Cleary came down from the High Road, hunched and unsteady like an old man, the collar of his overcoat turned up, pushing a thick brown scarf into his hair so dry and brittle that it might fall away like burnt string. His clothes seemed clean enough but somehow stale and his shoes were dirty. Against the soiled brick of the houses his face was a grey circle drawn with the infinite weariness of one whose mind is crawling from subconsciousness.

He paused, gathered himself, thought again of Hennessy's truck, looked back towards Manor House lights where it had flicked across his vision. It had been Hennessy's truck, battered and without sign-writing; he didn't miss things like that: Hennessy's truck north of the River, and Walworth was south. Nothing may be, but still to be remembered. The imminent thundering rage of Bredin at his lateness, that lay ahead, occupied him now, but only momentarily. The cold shrivelled him inside his clothes and he tried to hurry to the warmth of the office. Walking saved fares: it was two miles from McLeod to Bredin. Cleary watched pennies and pounds, and therein some-day ahead, he knew, was deliverance from all this. But how distant? Years, five, seven . . .

He was always late, a half hour, an hour, carefully at the edge of Bredin's tolerance. But it was almost midday now: he was three hours late. Christ! He had no depth of anxiety though; it was the physical torture of cold and lingering sleep that drove him on.

At the gate of the Repair Yard an apprentice shouted down from the cab of a truck, 'Ah ha, you dosser, you're wanked to a thread.'

'Look who's talking,' Cleary said: that was his rapier, a slow remembrance of school-yard cut and spit of ten years before.

'You're weak at the knees.'

'Not weak at the top.'

'Move on, wanker.'

'Look who's talking.'

He went up to the small wooden office at the top of the yard and pushed open the door. The pungent heat of the gas burner enveloped him like an overpowering pleasure. Only then did his lateness occur to him again and he rubbed his hands together and said to Bredin, 'You know, I awoke just after seven. And I felt like getting up then . . . '

'Are you awake now?' Bredin said very slowly. 'Are you sure? You look like a white maggot rolled up for the winter.'

'God, I don't know how it happens . . . when I awake early I feel like getting up . . . and then I drop off . . . '

He sat back against the warmth of the gas heater, smelling the sour steam from his coat; his buttocks glowed with the pleasure of it and a little shiver like sickness went through him: if he were

in bed now, drowsing and waking, listening for moments to the
traffic on the road down from Haringey and Manor House . . .
Hennessy's truck loomed across his mind again.

'You're on fire!' Bredin shouted at him, smelling the overheated cloth. 'You're on fire, you brainless ape!'

'Oh Jesus!' Cleary said; he slanted away from the heater, felt
his buttocks with both hands. The cloth was red-hot.

'Wake up! Wake up!'

Bredin went out and down the yard towards the workshops.
'Bloody blundering ape!' Cleary heard as the door slammed.

He went back and sat on the gas heater, angered a little.

The yard had the raw dampness of something new-born
about it; where feet had trodden, the frost was a black wetness.
Cleary looked out with distaste at it: stripped-down trucks
might never come to life again, he thought; a bulldozer with a
broken track and frozen clay caked in its entrails, a sludge
pump, a snake of collapsed hose, a giant concrete mixer and its
gaping drum like a shattered skull, crowded into the foreground.

Along the vista he watched the retreating form of Bredin.
Dosser! Bredin the dosser. Listen Bredin, you dosser, you have
something to say, spit it out. Don't say it when you're on the run
and the door is slamming. Have courage, boyo, stand here and
say it. You dosser, Bredin! He drifted away into the assuage-
ment of pain . . .

He heard the door open; it swung back against the metal
standards of a stores-rack and instantly he was prepared; the
explosion of anger, the footsteps coming across the room to
him, were nothing; he sank down behind the ramparts of his
helplessness and waited. Bredin was shouting '. . . I'll sack you
. . . sack you, you stupid little bastard! Do you hear? . . .' And
he waited with infinite patience.

When Bredin paused he pleaded with him. 'I don't feel so
good. In fact I thought of staying out today.'

Bredin stared at him.

'I thought I might see a doctor.'

'Oh Jesus,' Bredin said resignedly; anger seemed suddenly to
tire him.

'It's the strain over here.'

'The strain?'

'Three years over here,' Cleary said with hands held out for understanding and pity; as if there should be joy that he had so well withstood its ravages. 'Three years without a break. But I'll go home for Christmas.'

'Christ,' Bredin said with a frantic twitch of humour, 'won't that be grand.'

'Yes,' Cleary said.

'They can bury you with your breed.'

The resonance of Bredin's voice issued up from the hugeness of his stomach; there was pleasantness in it even when it clung to a string of profanity like black sump oil. He was old at fifty, tired and pulled into shapelessness with years of trudging over building sites, patching patched machinery, scraping the muck from it, belittling the hard swollen heads of foremen and gangers, and yet gripping the illusion that sometime, beyond some unexpected horizon, there would be satisfaction, a day when everything was right even for a little while. But could there be, he asked himself – when the world he had created was bleak – while big square hands were spawned each day? He saw them reaching out for the delicate precision of his machinery, to mangle it; he saw herds of big placid faces, deaf to the bone-dry hammer of pistons or the grind of a gear-box chipping itself down to size; faces without a tremor of pain.

'Get a list of the trucks,' he told Cleary. 'Check them against the sites.'

'I haven't been really well for months . . . '

'Shut your mouth,' Bredin told him.

Cleary took off his overcoat and went across to the table where he worked: his anger was only the ashes blowing from a dying fire, the faintest glow of orange. Bredin sat looking out the window at the cramped untidiness of the yard. He had a tin of black tobacco and cigarette papers.

When Bredin came on the cattle-boat, Cleary thought, only the scrapings and gaol-birds came: a little spleen had crept up and was ready for its careful expression.

'I saw Hennessy's truck at Manor House,' he said. 'Just now, at Manor House.'

'It must have run you over, by Christ!'

'He's at Walworth.'

Bredin was silent.

'A bit far from home, isn't he?'

'He was here at seven for a speedo.'

'Five hours,' Cleary said almost inaudibly, seemingly without motive. 'A long time ago.'

'He was here at seven, last night's load still on his springs. He'd go to shoot at Rye House or beyond, wouldn't he? Where were you at seven?'

Bredin gazed into the graveyard of his machinery and was thoughtful; he went out again and Cleary looked after him; scattered drops of frosty rain smeared the windows. Bredin came from nothing, he thought; all his life over here, when there was hardly food or money: the lean fifties had spawned an army of half-baked chancers.

He went back to sit on the gas heater, almost slept now in the overloaded air, drifted away from the impingement of everything. Bredin's heavy step was lost to him but when the door opened he was instinctively groping his way from the heater to the chair.

The voice he heard was too fragile, he knew; unsteady; he could sense deep anger in it.

'I haven't been really well for months . . . '

'Listen . . . listen . . . Oh Christ Jesus give me patience! . . . Listen, you poor miserable dosser, if you left yourself alone, if you washed yourself, if you wore clean clothes, if you went out every week for your pint and a woman you might with time begin to look human. But you're a festering boar poked out of his sleep.'

'I'm not well, I tell you.'

'Since when?'

'Three, four months.'

'You looked as dirty and as stupid the day you stepped in the gate.'

Bredin gazed at his face and wondered at the slow agonised thoughts that must be behind it: the hands were like his mind, pale and dirty, always hovering without purpose. He kept him because, incredibly, he loved him a little; like a deformed child. Nally had sent him of course: it was Nally's money: there might be a plan or a purpose somewhere but Bredin left intrigue at the doorstep; he was tired, no one's man.

'Have you money?' he asked suddenly.

'Well . . . not much . . . '

'Here's a quid. Go down to the caff and eat something. And get yourself shaved.' He gave him another pound. 'You look like the bottom of a pig trough.'

'Yes . . . yes . . . I'll go now.'

'And wake yourself up!' Bredin hammered the table in front of him. 'If I catch you idle again today I'll fire you. Do you hear? By Christ in heaven, I'll kick you out the gate!'

Cleary sidled past him, rubbing his mouth in penitence, and made a little show of hurry down the yard. Bredin liked that, he knew; he'd like to think he had a lame dog to bully and feed and lock up and set free. Stupid dosser.

Cleary saw him at the end of his delicate cast, played out, imperceptibly drawn to the shore.

'Don't hurry now,' the apprentice on the truck at the gate said. 'You'll be tired out for this evening.'

'Your jaw-bone will be tired out.'

He went down the quiet street towards the caff, breathless in cold. He would take an hour to himself now; first at the barber's, then in the sweltering heat of the caff he would have rolls and hot steaming tea . . .

Free food, he thought for a moment, and salary while he ate it: being a fool had only little hardships. Nally, he suddenly wondered, Nally who paid them all, even Bredin . . . he had never seen him.

Nally had been sitting with his morning post when Hennessy had rung: site reports from gangers, foremen, from Feehan too; sales sheets of liquor, tobacco, bar food; fruit-machine take; commissions; weekly bank statements of property rents in. Nally's properties were crumbling freehold tenements cultivated to rot and disintegrate by neglect. Only the ground interested Nally: he might build again, or sell if the price was right. And there was a stocktaker's report that he would look at again: little peaks and drops were tell-tale as temperature charts. A youth club where once he had punched and skipped about was having a whip-round and he wrote a cheque for fifty pounds . . .

It took more than an hour to deal with it and clear his desk. It was moving for twelve. He rang McLeod.

'I'm glad I caught you,' he said. 'A bit of bother.'

'Ah.'

'I'll be at Maida Vale in an hour, give or take. Can you make it?'

'Of course.'

'Good.'

He remained sitting before the polished wood of his desk, the pale green blotter; he heard the sound of a food machine from the kitchens, and water flowing in a bathroom made a faint vibrant drone in the ancient walls of his room.

He rang and Helena came. 'I'll be out for quite a while,' he told her. He touched her hair and kissed her. 'You look perfect,' he said.

She brought his coat, hat, gloves from the wardrobe, turned up the collar of the Burberry, left the belt a little awry. He judged the soft shapeless rake of the tweed hat himself.

She nodded approval.

'No problems?' he asked.

'I'll miss you.'

'Of course.'

As he went down the broad stairway he thought he could hear her almost silent amusement. The stair treads had polished wooden edges, carpet centrepiece, old brass finialled stair-rods. Helena's discipline shone everywhere, in the strange happenstance warmth of dining-room, bar, lounge, in the undisturbed years of everything. Nally had once watched her skill here and there, over a year or more, bringing style and cuisine to ungifted slags and soirées, coming and going with a kind of magic self-effacement. And he had snapped her up. Helena's hotel was a kind of flagship.

He liked everything she did. Only the central heating was a little offensive – inevitably – and his own rooms were free of it.

He moved out and briskly down the winter hill of etched stone, roadside trees black as wire; the cold air seemed to sculpt him, face and garments, from the grey-blue substance of the sky. At Highgate station he turned downhill towards Archway and the roar of traffic was tireless: dinosaurs had returned, he thought, with man-made racketing diesel hearts and rectal tubes in endless thunder. He was happier now, stepping out, looking at the vastness of the sky, touched for a moment only with self-assessment and the peril of humility.

Archway roundabout, with its island rookery pub, was a monster centrifuge of wheels and tumult, and he went down to the subways, still freshborn but already defaced, vandalised, pissed-on, at evening time more fraught than the Great North Road and Upper Street of the highwaymen. He was contemplating the little problem of Hennessy and how he would handle McLeod. He took a taxi at Junction Road.

The Club at Maida Vale was nameless; its members and friends knew its co-ordinates and that was sufficient. It was a large basement and a few stone steps gave access to a polished door: a plate was engraved 'Number twenty-six'. Nally selected a key and entered the hallway. Muzak, the spill of conversation, coins tinkling from a fruit-machine: the mixed sounds just reached him.

The minder stood, raised a finger in salutation, smiled carefully. He took Nally's coat, hat, gloves.

'I'm expecting someone. Show him up, won't you?'

Ahead was the entrance to the bar and its amenities; beside him, a private curtained archway, where Nally passed through, climbed a half-dozen steps to a room of leather comfort and quiet scattered lighting. His camera he sometimes called it, where unseen, in total silence, he could look down on the movement, restless as a sea, the ebb and flow of drink and cash. He could sit there in company or in undisturbed reverie. Down below too for the punters was a television hide; and a betting slips runner to man the blower, make the odds – ten per cent, Nally. Ten per cent at the 'book-shop' too. Twenty per cent was fair, Nally thought: on a lazy race-day he could take a ton for starters. He watched the waves break endlessly on the bar.

In a little while McLeod came; tall, thin, not strong: the mild face of a scholar, scarce silky hair once fair but dulling now, a good sheepskin, nothing else worth a glance. The minder brought iced Perry and thick slices of lemon.

Nally said, 'Yes, our man, as you put it, was over-qualified.'

'Jumped the gun?'

'Made a move this morning. Week ahead.'

'Yes.'

'You heard?'

'Local radio, just a mention. Eighty-four thousand. Not a lot these days. Irish, they thought.'

McLeod's deep growling voice hardly belonged in so refined a frame.

'Yes,' Nally said; he looked down at the restless world, the coloured notes pushed to and fro on the beaten copper surface of the counter, the smiling barmaids, the slender hands. The manager, unobtrusive, moved here and there as if merely to nod and smile.

'Eighty-four?'

'Yes.'

'He wants it down the middle.'

'Yes. It was unusual, you see, the one-man thing, daredevil stuff . . . '

'Newsworthy,' Nally said.

'He did well.'

'Time will tell.'

'He's not run of the mill, is he?'

'Over here at fifteen? . . .' Nally thought about it and said humourlessly for McLeod, 'Boarding school boy, I'd have a guess, big bulge in his jockstrap, home on hols with a hard-on, gives the grocer's missus one, maybe poles the parson's daughter too, pisses off. Sin is very important in Ballymackduckpond or Dead Man's Gulch at the time of speaking, you know.'

'Or Stoke Poges,' McLeod said.

They sat in silence, sipped the iced water sharp with lemon. They would agree precisely on what must be done and sitting in silence a while was a kind of gesture of camaraderie, trust, good faith. There was a phone on the table. Nally rang the manager downstairs and watched him move smiling to the counter.

'Yes?'

'The old crow on the bandit,' Nally said.

'Yes?'

'Dud fifty-pees in the change-slot. Plays now and then. Old hand. Softly, softly, of course. A member?'

'Yes.'

'Recent is she?'

'Yes.'

'Leave word at the door. Next time she comes he'll explain. And send us a drink.'

McLeod smiled. 'Inexplicably' the lights in the bandit flickered and failed, 'Out of order' was hung on its dead face. The pleasant little coiffured lady bought a double gin with a handful of coins.

'Hennessy. You can leave this whole matter to me, I think. I'll keep in touch.'

McLeod nodded.

'Thieves we have every day. Clapped out old gammers down there. Managers, gaffers, gangers, foremen, navvies too. Knock the till, hit and run, fiddle the bandits, plant a "dead man" here and there, mix miles and gallons, take what you can. Write-offs, draw a line, that's all. Not worth chasing. Someone will see them of course. I arrange that. Break a head or good teeth or a jaw. Or a leg if it's bad enough. And word gets round . . .'

'Yes.'

'But we don't write off a big piece, do we?'

McLeod was silent.

'Or send someone?'

'No.'

'It has to be quiet, very quiet. I'll handle Hennessy myself.'

'He's putting up half, of course.'

'Yes,' Nally said. 'That's a start.'

The manager came with a bottle of port and dry biscuits. 'I'm sorry about the fruit machine,' he said.

'Don't worry about it,' Nally told him.

When he had gone McLeod said, 'Feehan at Paddington? . . .'

'I'll be coming to that,' Nally said. 'But you're happy about the Hennessy bit?'

'Oh yes.'

'I could send a visitor, give him a limp, fingers pointing arse about face, set him up like a puff of smoke even. But this is different. We want something tidy.'

'Yes.'

Nally telephoned Walworth and Feehan answered.

'How do you find things?'

'Fair.'

'But moving along?'

'Yes.'

'That heading-driver, what do you call him?'

'Kirwan.'

'Keep him in a sweat, won't you?'

'Yes.'

'Hennessy? Truck driver.' Nally looked across to McLeod; he could sense Feehan's anxiety. 'Hennessy, I said.'

'Air-lock, busted speedo, that kind of story. Muck tipped out beyond Broxbourne this morning.'

'But he's on site?'

'Came late.'

'Many loads?'

'Gone with the first.'

'Mmmmm,' Nally said. 'You could be right, might be a clever bastard. Very expensive muck, you see?'

'Yes.'

'Put him on your list.'

'Yes.'

'Very expensive.' Nally drank his port, let Feehan worry a little. 'I've spent a morning on costs,' he said eventually. 'Black spots here and there, too many really.'

'Walworth?'

'Yes. Keep down on it, won't you?'

Feehan was mumbling something.

Nally said, 'The flat at Paddington needs paint, I think. And the furniture? Three-piece, isn't it? Grotty, if I remember. We'll change it.'

37

'Well,' Feehan said dutifully. 'It isn't urgent.'

'I've picked up a few decent things,' Nally said. 'Dump the three-piece tonight. Yes, get Hennessy to call for it. Late. Seven thirty, say. Forget to book his hours, you know? Ride him hard a while.' He could hear Feehan's noise of approval. 'And stay with Walworth a day or two. I might call to see you.'

He hung up; McLeod was nodding satisfaction.

'I think you see what's in mind?'

'Very good,' McLeod said.

'We'll stretch our legs here a while, wait for dark, and go down to your . . .'

'My studio, I call it,' McLeod said. 'You'll find it's quite comfortable.'

It was after five, blowing dry powdered snow, when they took a taxi from Maida Vale.

McLeod's studio had once, no doubt, been a withdrawing-room of some taste and elegance but only the plaster centrepiece and edge mouldings of the ceiling remained of more prestigious times. It was comfortable, as he had said. The curtains on two large windows were already drawn and he switched on a fire and a table lamp. It was a studio: tripods, cameras, floods, filters, screens; and on the walls, blow-ups of matt landscapes, ageing streets, nudes, children, animals.

The entrance was from a service laneway at the rear, through a littered garden, up an iron staircase to his door.

Nally was pleased with it.

'Humbuggery, most of it,' McLeod said. 'Cameras, just shells. Except this one.'

It stood not more than thirty inches from the floor, aimed at a curtained window. McLeod switched out fire and light, pushed back the curtains for a few seconds, raised the window perhaps three inches. The camera pointed its long white metal nose across the street, through the darkness, to the steps and door-way of Feehan's flat. It was loaded and set.

'Seven thirty Hennessy comes, you said?'

'About then.'

McLeod closed the window, the curtains, restored light and heat.

'I have some brandy,' he said.

'Fine.'

'This morning you mentioned tidying up.'

'It's time, I think.'

'Good idea,' McLeod said. 'Things are finished here. Houses don't stay safe for long. The runners know that. A year or two. It's had its fling, good pictures, faces to follow. But, winding down, almost gone . . .'

Nally nodded. 'Get Hennessy in your book and give me a day or two,' he said.

'We'll know where he is, will we?'

'Yes. I have a kip at Archway. He dosses there. That Kirwan fellow too.'

The flow of traffic from London Bridge, and the bridges at Blackfriars and the Tower, and the upward surges from Brixton, Camberwell and the Old Kent Road, make a great oily turbulence at the Elephant and Castle. The Elephant roundabouts, like magic rings, are linked to take every dizzy current and counter-flow. Walworth Road, a spin-off, is never silent.

From the site office on a bulldozed patch Feehan looked out at the frozen ground: machines, cranes, piled muck, ballast, brick hardcore; men, deep in trenches, trimming sides, close-timbering, holding back the crushing weight with walings and struts and pages. He had a face of unrelieved ugliness as if it had been cast in a high constricted mould. Everything was wrong, like a bizarre photofit. He was tall and long-armed; his fists were dense bone hammer-heads.

He looked at the site-office phone and remembered each word of Nally's conversation. Nally never made friendly sounds but even the absence of chill was a burning sunlight. Feehan felt strangely commended: Kirwan on his list, Hennessy too; a face-lift and furniture for Paddington. It was a good day.

But it was near winding-up time now, with winter darkness, turned half past four, and Hennessy was still out on his first haul. Feehan looked at the frozen ridges of muck along the trench-lines, white-capped, snow-dusted, like breaking waves; and, about Kirwan's shaft, the fresh clay of his day's efforts and the rock-solid ring of yesterday's dig awaiting Hennessy. He arranged the fawn executive duffel, his actor's hat, and stepped out. Very expensive muck, Nally had said.

The shaft to Kirwan's tunnel had a twenty-foot drop, and a site-crane, like a little maternal bird, leant over it. Feehan stood on the gathered muck and looked down at the shining clay floor. The timbered sides had a cowboy shanty look about them, but it took skill to dig yourself down to twenty feet and timber as you went. On your back or belly then to drive the four-by-three horizontal tunnel in darkness or in the half-light of a storm lamp, and leave it too timbered and shored behind you. Miss or skimp and it was a grave.

But Feehan saw only muck: the fresh and wet measured Kirwan's day and the frozen piles were Hennessy's backlog. Fingers in teeth, he whistled down the shaft for Kirwan, hammered with a pickhead on the steel skip of the crane beside him. Kirwan's grey head came warily out of the heading and peered up.

'Come up, Kirwan, come up, boy, come up!'

There was a vertical ladder lashed to the walings; Kirwan dragged his weary pile of overweight from rung to rung. He arrived grey and puffed, an old man.

'Muck at the face?'

'Half a skip, maybe.'

'Get it up here boy.'

'Jesus,' Kirwan said, open-mouthed like a fish, 'it takes an hour to bring a skip of muck off the face. The crane driver knows when to come.'

'The crane driver is gone,' Feehan said. Like a horse-trader he looked deep into Kirwan's face and neck and shoulders. 'He was old, Kirwan, a bit dodgy, you know. Expensive, you could say. You can do his bit too.'

'Christ!' Kirwan said. 'That little terrified rabbit, you chopped him, you bastard!'

'You could be next.' Feehan nodded at the crane. 'Start it up.'

In long moments Kirwan measured him for bloody battle,

40

and then suddenly he was thinking of Hennessy in the morning's distant room, and caution, reluctant, bitter, held him in check. He thought of Maisie too who would be shocked, agape, in tears maybe, to see him summoned like a dog, near enough kicked.

'Move, Kirwan, you stupid bastard!'

Kirwan climbed on the platform, started the crane, swung out the steel skip and lowered it to the floor of the shaft; he followed it down, almost slumping from rung to rung. As he got on his knees to crawl inside the gloom of the tunnel he could hear Feehan shouting, 'Fingers out now, dryballs! . . . Fingers out . . . ' and he moved on towards the face.

He hadn't seen Hennessy, only his tyre marks; Hennessy had been on site, he knew, and was gone for the tip out beyond the marshes at Plumstead. He had been breathless, a little dizzy, with relief, looking at the deep wheel tracks where Hennessy had pulled away . . .

He rested a moment now in the long coffin of the heading, looked at the wet ooze of muck before him, the drip of slime from between the timbers. Hennessy had sidestepped it, given it a miss: you didn't tangle, fling your hat in the ring with the Nallys and run free! A glow of thanksgiving warmed Kirwan's aching bones: the morning seemed a flimsy sweaty dream, listening to the fading sounds of Hennessy's truck, remembering Maisie, the bus stop . . .

The muck from the face was piled on a length of tarpaulin tied like a hammock at its ends. Kirwan dragged it out into the light; Feehan's ridicule stung like metal. He shovelled from tarpaulin to skip until, with a drag of stomach and groin, he could heave the rest over the navel-high rim before him.

'Come on! . . . Come on!'

Jesus, he thought, on the pain of the ladder, looking up at the end of a winter's day: Hennessy was right, Hennessy was right. He was on the crane again, drawing up the skip, slewing it to the edge of the shaft; he looked for the pickhead to hammer the tight latch of the skip and let the muck topple on the deck. But it was lost. Feehan was beside him, looking at the wet sludge of his day. 'I'll tape you tomorrow. A good man always likes the tape, doesn't he, young fellow? You'll earn a crust before the week is out or I'll leave a toe up your arsehole.'

The sweat of drink and age was on Kirwan's face; he studied the small smears of muck on Feehan's polished shoes, the sharp crease of trouser legs, the smart duffel, the shirt and tie, the grey eyes, the dancing master's hat. He left the loaded skip there, shook his head and began to climb down to the silence of his grave again.

Feehan watched the grey head out of sight and went on tour. He moved from cluster to cluster, leaving a broadcast of resentment behind him, but prodded everywhere, made capital of anger and rancour. Near five Hennessy came.

'Where were you, mister?'

'Abbeywood.'

'That's one load today.'

'Right.'

'Try four tomorrow.'

Hennessy said, 'Make ten miles a hour from here to Plumstead, you're good.'

'Well, tomorrow you'll have to be very good, won't you, mister?'

Hennessy waited. 'Is that all?'

'No,' Feehan said. 'Tonight. Put it on your logsheet, mister. Half seven on the pip, I'll want you. My place at Paddington. You know it. A few sticks of furniture I want dumped. Half seven, I said . . . not before . . . not after . . .'

Hennessy moved away. The day was done: young faces, drawn, dirty, faded into the evening, to pubs or rooms or Christ knows where, left behind them the site with steel pins and plastic tape. The machines were silent, the flashing lamps in place. Feehan drove his car to the edge of the kerb and nosed into the traffic.

And Hennessy stood and searched the pavements and doorways for signs of Nally or his minders. There was nothing. All afternoon he had watched, on the road to Plumstead and back, stalled and watched and pulled and stalled and watched again. There had been nothing; nothing to jar the changeless rote of another day . . .

He saw Kirwan come up from his shaft and drag tired hurrying feet over muck and rubble.

Kirwan faced him. 'Well?'

'Well what?' Hennessy said.

'You pulled out, didn't you, eh? You're here, thank Christ for that! Jesus, I want a couple of pints of beer in my tank, then I'll move!'

'No pubs yet,' Hennessy said. He had whiskey; he handed him the half-bottle and watched him slug at it: one, two, three ...; they sat in the hammer of the truck cab and turned north for the River. 'You have no money or fags, have you,' Hennessy said. He gave him a pack with three or four in it. 'It was quiet here today, was it?'

Kirwan was silent behind a cloud of warmth and smoke. At London Bridge he said, 'What was the balls-up? You had a rush of common sense, had you?'

'You don't have to worry about me,' Hennessy said.

'Worry!' Kirwan whispered at him. 'I have a pain in my gut since the first crack of light and Feehan, that dead-faced bastard, up my arse. We do another week here, no more. And move. You hear?'

'Yes,' Hennessy said. 'You told Feehan this morning, did you? Like I said.'

'I told him.'

'He's on site all day. What's up?'

'Maybe the muck's too dear.' Kirwan looked at him. 'Or the heading. Our turn for the stick, the lash, the boot, a shower of fucks everywhere. The crane man's down the road, a few more with him. The tape for me tomorrow, dear Christ!' Kirwan laughed in the boost of whiskey. 'Another week, Hennessy.'

On the long push to Archway, through Bishopsgate and Shoreditch, Manor House, the fringes of Hornsey, Hennessy broke the silence once.

'I'm on for Feehan tonight,' he said. 'Furniture to be dumped.'

Kirwan laughed again, suddenly, like a bark. 'Christ, that's a new one! Feehan's furniture!'

'Isn't it?' Hennessy said. 'You could call it strange even.'

But Kirwan wasn't listening; warmed in alcohol and the

43

long drags of tobacco he still made sounds of amusement; he watched the wiper blades gathering sleet and rubbed his palm on the clouded window. 'He fancies you, he'll pay you well,' he said.

They parked in the backwaters of Archway. Kirwan stopped. He said quietly to Hennessy, 'I'm glad you jacked it, you were on a loser.' They walked up to their street of tall thin houses reduced to beggary and Kirwan pointed at them. 'Dirty kips, aren't they?' he said. 'But well ahead of a cage at the bridewell . . .'

Turned half six, Cleary stood at the bus stop; people came and went. Sometimes with a rolled newspaper he beat a little gentle tattoo on his palm, breathed out the smoky vapour of gathering cold. He could look upstreet and across at the dark window of Hennessy's doss. Empty? But Hennessy's truck was parked round the corner. Cleary felt a little excitement. There was a minicab shop behind him and sometimes he stood in the door's embrasure to hide from the edge of the breeze. Patience was a badge.

He glanced at his paper again. Down in the scrags of its page three he read, 'Herts Hold-up Haul'. And ' . . . bandit's brogue, skipping schoolgirls, Bulldog Briggs defiant . . . eighty thousand'.

He looked again at the dark window, walked a little to peer for Hennessy's truck in the gloom of a side-street. It stood there, the frost gathering on its windscreen.

It had been strange to crawl up to Manor House at the end of a morning and catch – almost lose! – that single frame of Hennessy whipped away in the traffic. The time was right too, and a broken speedo cable . . .

Hot from Herts, more like it, he composed, loaded with loot: a whole new web-work for McLeod!

It was a moment of triumph, he felt instinctively sure. And suddenly then the thought took shape, terrifyingly at that instant, that he was alone with his knowledge, in charge. Bredin, McLeod, Hennessy, were hardly aware of him moving

44

at the fringes of their worlds. He had discovered Hennessy himself.

He looked at his image in the stacked window of a junk-shop: the hunched shoulders, the paper, rolled, clamped to his ribs like a comic swagger-stick. In the bitter tears of the wind his infant courage was returning.

Eighty thousand, a whole jackpot, fearfully he envisioned it lining his battered suitcase at Highbury, for a year, longer perhaps, as long as was necessary, never a penny spent until it was time, unobtrusively, to take his leave, wave adieu to McLeod, vanish without trace. Bredin's clerk, wanker Cleary, nark for McLeod, boar poked out of his sleep. And now there was a winning post. He felt almost ill.

Then suddenly, again, he was overcome with fear, terror, and he trembled, felt a moment of incontinence and a warm drip of urine on his thighs. He walked the stretch of pavement up and down, rubbing away at the dampness . . .

From his room, its vacant stare, a few feet back from the window, Hennessy watched him. It was freezing: the frost shone on the pavements and in the wells of light from the street lamps and noise was sharper. He heard Kirwan, out on the landing, saying, 'You're not in that hurry. Come on in and smoke a fag with us.'

'I couldn't, Bill.'

'Come on, come on!'

'I'm going to Cricklewood.' Maisie's voice was sweet and childlike.

'You're not?' Kirwan said with a great show of amazement.

'Starting tonight.'

'God Almighty!' Kirwan was orating. 'Why didn't you let me know? Why?' Hennessy could hear him clapping his hands on his buttocks in despair. 'You should have told me. You knew I'd want to be there.'

. . . Hennessy had seen Cleary arriving, watched him without pause in his gauche careless movements, like a penny-dreadful spy shiveringly studying himself, and oddments of all things, in the chaos of a junk-shop, standing at a bus shelter until every service had passed him twice: a little comedy figure flopping around in the melodrama. Bredin? Bredin wouldn't waste time or temper putting tags on two-a-penny drivers: they suited him or they didn't.

Before now Cleary had peered at him often, Hennessy knew, with a kind of half-awakened interest, watching and drowsing like an old beaten sheepdog from behind his table at Bredin's Yard. But down there on the pavement was a thread of purpose somewhere, even in each overplayed gesture of secrecy, as if the little greasy manikin had been programmed and pushed out into the evening.

Hennessy sat on the edge of his bed and remembered lunch-time and the Manor House lights and the instant of Cleary flitting across his vision: whatever tangled scheme was afoot might have had its beginnings there. He remembered his caution and felt again the tightness of it, and uncertainty hovered: if Cleary wasn't launched from Bredin's slip-leash, whose moth-eaten bloodhound was he? Forty-odd thousand in Kirwan's pile of rot and maggots next door; and a hundred yards from Cleary on the pavements, in the truck, untended, under the driving seat, another neat corded parcel. He stood and looked down again at the insignificance of Cleary in the piercing bitterness of the evening. Cleary, an outlandish mess-enger for Nally's share? A tumble into farce! Not even with barge poles or by infinitely long threads would Nally manipu-late the foot-soldiers and snitches.

Hennessy looked at the gun still at his waist since Briggs had charged, and it had rested against the white leather of Henderson's neck. He felt the warmth of it. It was after seven o'clock. Feehan's job at Paddington clanged like a broken bell: it was wrong, a jangle. He put on an overcoat and scarf.

On the landing Kirwan called out, 'Good luck now, love. And thanks, Maisie . . . thanks. I'll be there one way or another.'

When he came in, Hennessy said, 'You touched her for money.'

'Before God, I didn't,' Kirwan said. 'Before my God. What do you take me for? She gave it to me, shoved it down into my pocket. Listen, wait till you hear.'

'You make six times what she earns.'

'She's playing tonight.'

'I heard.' Hennessy began carefully to arrange his movements.

'Cricklewood,' Kirwan said. 'A fair pub, you know.' Its prominence and Maisie's music might have been his personal achievements. He sat on Hennessy's bed.

Hennessy said, 'Feehan's pub too. You can send him a drink.'

'Bollicks to Feehan. Give us a fag.'

'I thought you had some.'

'I haven't.'

'You were inviting Maisie in to smoke mine?'

'Oh for Christ's sake give us a fag and don't make a song about it.' He took out Maisie's money and crushed it into a ball in his hand. 'I'll be getting fags in a few minutes.'

Growing old and the mannerisms of youth, a little sadly, clashed again: he should be the foreman now with a house in Kilburn and a fat wife and lodgers to pay the rent and beer bills. But time had always fled past Kirwan.

Hennessy gave him the cigarette and saw the urge for movement in his eyes; he wanted to be rushing away to Cricklewood, sending up a drink to Maisie on the stage, hovering about her at the intervals. Only the flimsiness of bank-roll, hardly a shot in the locker, halted him. Maisie was a kind of kin and security for him with her teenage voice and mannerisms and growing a little threadbare in youth like himself.

'She looked special tonight,' he said: he thought of her warm frilly room on the ground floor and times he had tapped on her door when the house was asleep, the slow turning of his key, the door opening inch and inch and Maisie's voice, 'Who is it?'

'I couldn't sleep, Maisie. True as God, I couldn't sleep.'

They had often lain there in the darkness and warmth listening to the last buses pushing for home; he remembered she had said once, 'You're a fine man, Kirwan, a fine man.' The rain had been coming down in torrents outside and they had heard the lonely swish of late traffic on the High Road . . .

'Don't light that fag yet,' Hennessy said.

Kirwan looked at him, motionless, in the kind of frying texture of gloom. The old brass light-socket was empty. 'Some gobshite nicked your bulb. That gin-bag in the basement is a caretaker, isn't she? In bed or the boozer and her door on the swing when she goes for a bender. Too tired to climb this high.'

'And see the pile of crap in your corner?' Hennessy said. 'She takes rent, that's all.'

Kirwan fumbled with matches again.

'No lights.'

'Oh for Christ's sake!' Kirwan groaned.

'You know Bredin's clerk, do you? You've seen him, small with a sleepy hump and misses nothing.'

Hennessy beckoned and wearily Kirwan came across.

'Near the bus-stop.'

Kirwan nodded. 'It could be.'

'He's there a while.'

'Unless he flashes it or touches up the female fuzz he could be there for a week. It's a free country.' Kirwan went back to the bedside, flopped there, held up the cigarette for permission.

'Wait,' Hennessy said.

Kirwan gazed at the white pillar of tobacco, his scarred misshapen hands; fingers, unfinished stumps of a backyard sculptor, skin that would never be clean or nails unbroken. He smelt the sour muck of the shaft again and the long grave of his tunnel. The polished shoes with the faintest smears of muck, he remembered, and the actor's hat.

'Feehan's furniture . . . ' Hennessy was saying.

Kirwan seemed to awaken. 'I'll kill that bastard, you know.'

Hennessy nodded him to silence. His own regret or unhappiness was down beyond his fatigue; it was bitterly cold; across the rooftops, he thought, the world seemed old and tattered with being snatched from hand to hand.

Kirwan said, 'Feehan. Set a mick to kick a mick. Tight as a drum, mean as a dosser's kip.' He was a little breathless, hungry for the drag of smoke and its taste filling his mind. 'But he'll play ball with the hard-nuts all right.'

'The hard-nuts?' Hennessy said.

'I need a smoke for Christ's sake!' He saw the light bulb on Hennessy's pillow and picked it up. 'What's the darkness about?'

'What about Feehan?'

'Listen!' Kirwan groaned his impatience. 'I know a latch at

Willesden Junction chats the mots at weekends, puts up the beer, says he guns every hoor in Harlesden. And he'd run at the lift of a brasser's bib. Shadow of a gunman, they call him ...'

'What about Feehan?'

'Like that only different, see?' He left time for Hennessy to think about it. 'Half a hard-man, all an arsehole, a one-night doss for the hard-nut croppies. A shadow.'

'Feehan?'

The pieces shifted uncomfortably in Hennessy's mind, made broken pictures, slipped away out of focus, out of control. Feehan: a Paddington bolt-hole for skins on the trot.

'A lot of balls!' he said, to fill the silence.

'Maybe,' Kirwan said. 'Down on your back in a tunnel, a priest in his box, you know, words come in from the daylight up there. I hear it all. Traffic sounds, the crunch of feet. And words. Everything far away but clear as a bell. Sites are always whispering.' He looked for a long time at Hennessy. 'You're in bother, aren't you?'

'No.'

Feehan, Hennessy was thinking: set a mick to catch a mick. Simple, crude, dangerous, unpaid, not Nally's stamp at all. There was something else beyond his reach and he groped for it. 'Light your fag on the landing,' he said, and when Kirwan came back, 'A little job for you now.'

'I'm for Cricklewood.' Kirwan opened his fist on Maisie's crumpled notes.

'Two pints and a packet of fags won't get you far.' Hennessy gave him a twenty and his keys. 'You could move my truck a block or so and not wake the watcher down there, couldn't you?'

'Wait!'

Hennessy nodded down at Cleary crouched in a doorway. 'Park up, double back here, get on his tracks! No truck, he'll move off soon. Find out where he hangs.'

'Maisie ... ' Kirwan began, a little confused and uncertain now; he needed the warmth of whiskey.

'A drink?'

Hennessy took the half-bottle from his pocket and gave it to him, watched him drain it.

'It could take all night.'

Hennessy shook his head. 'An hour, maybe. Come back.'

Kirwan considered it behind a winter smile. 'You're a clever bastard, Hennessy.' He waited. 'I should know something, shouldn't I?'

'A parcel in the driver's seat. When you get back put it in Maisie's place.'

'Maisie's!'

'You have a key.'

'Christ, you can't lumber Maisie!'

'And take the truck to Cricklewood. Give Maisie a lift home.'

'Listen!'

'And don't get pissed!'

Hennessy walked him to the landing, faced him.

'I wouldn't lumber you or Maisie, would I?'

Kirwan stared, closed his eyes in deathlike weariness.

'Would I?'

'No.'

'We're home and dry. A few days, that's all. And shake this crap off our feet.'

Kirwan looked at the bare treads of the stairs, weeping walls, plaster sagging like ageing flesh. 'Home and dry?'

Hennessy nodded.

'And Feehan?'

'It's a bad night for furniture. I'll pay him a call though.'

'Take care.'

'Yes,' Hennessy said. 'I'll take care.'

He listened to Kirwan's footsteps on the stairs and in the hallway.

He went back to his room, put the bulb in its socket but kept the last minutes of his vigil in darkness . . .

A bus halted, the driver took fares. In its lee he saw Kirwan slip into the evening, turn off to round the block on the blind side of Cleary. It would take ten minutes, maybe less.

Hennessy switched on his light, then from the deep gloom of Kirwan's next-door doss he watched Cleary come alive. Head down, eyes alert like a wary hen, Cleary hired a minicab, sat in wait for lights out and the pursuit of Hennessy . . .

Minutes slid past, cold seemed to grow in the silence; Kirwan's maggoty pile of rubbish was untouched.

When Kirwan surfaced again, advancing on the pavements, it was time to go.

Hennessy crossed the landing, tightened his coat about him, flicked his own room back to darkness, for a moment or two watched Cleary's mini move him down, ready to stalk the quarry already flown.

Hennessy reached the pavements. He glanced back to see Cleary in altercation, in flight, hands to buttocks, from the cabbie's polyglot flux of profanity; and Kirwan steadily on his trail.

Hennessy caught a black taxi near Tufnell Park Station and sat back on the hard upholstery, in shadow.

The gathered weariness of weeks, months, capsulated, blurred in memory, drew apace with him, he thought. Fourteen hours a day on how many battle-grounds? Muck, load it, tip it, quids for loads, never enough; weariness, a pale undulant fever; muck-men down in the trenches, hired by the yard, shiny in sweat; a roar of compressors, the long air-lines, jack-hammers, shining steels thundering into the frozen ground, the shovels rising; the stale sweaty rooms they lived in, the liquid muck ankle-deep down in the open-cuts, the split fingers and broken nails.

It seemed a long fairytale journey to Highgate . . .

They were moving into the Harrow Road junction now, over a music hall's untended grave, the long-dead scrumpy dens and knocking-shops, past the police station's fearful neo-geometry and on to Paddington Green, dimly lit as if wartime gloom had never left it, the statue of Sarah Siddons frozen gracelessly, more dimmed in memory than Polly Perkins, where once there was a trolley bus turn, a mobile caff, drivers with fags and cuppas.

They pushed into the languishing Georgian flair at the fringes of Bayswater, a world of dead squares and crescents: a thousand one-room flats with grease marks and flaking walls, the drip of clothes on floors, awful infant wails of protest at the sanctity of life. The taxi's radio had a hoarse blow-lamp silence, a death-rattle, and sudden bursts of echoing gibberish like moon-talk.

Hennessy leant forward and gave instructions. It was a long backwater street, an empty converging drive between tall pedimented houses, sad century-old distinctions still clinging to them: now a fading chimney-sweep's sign hung down from an ironwork marquise, window balconies sagged, the graffiti jungle sprawled across magnificent pilasters.

'You get near half-way down, slow a bit,' Hennessy said. 'Not too much.' He measured the run with door numbers. 'I need a look as we go, that's all. A flat. But it smells end of the world, a kip.'

'All this, one big knocking-shop,' the taximan said . . .

Approaching, passing Feehan's door, Hennessy from deep in shadow scanned the houses opposite. He saw a first-floor window raised a little, inches only, and the street lights barely reached what might be rot or splashy posters on a screen, a wall. A moment and the diorama had spun.

'That's OK,' he told the driver. There was still a bleak stretch of road beyond. 'Swing out to the shops. Anywhere then.'

The taxi left him at the Chippenham on the Harrow Road again where it draws in for Kensal Green, He saw a minicab shop but wanted time and a drink first: the whole tight plan was in motion, slipping from him. Even in the cold air he was dry and for a moment hectic as fever. He drank a pint of beer, lingered at the end of his glass . . .

If Kirwan had it right, there was another villainy about. Feehan: a two-inch slot of open window facing him on a bitter night? Guests and callers recorded, maybe, Hennessy thought. Furniture men too? The image was blurred, amorphous, characters faceless or not at all. He had to be sure who sat in the darkness logging Feehan's doorstep traffic.

He took a mini back to the mouth of the long canyon road, parked, sat in front with a pale Jamaican driver. Time was wasting.

'Might be a long job.'

'That's all right, man. You're not the fuzz, I see.'

'Not the fuzz,' Hennessy said.

'That's for sure.' The driver's teeth shone in the half-light. 'Nice soft hands, polished nails for the fuzz.' He looked at Hennessy's knuckles, battered skin, nails and laughed.

In a little while Hennessy gave him Feehan's door number. 'Half-way up,' he said. 'Walk past but spot the other side. There's an open window, only a crack. Move smart, it's cold, like you're going somewhere, you know? To the end and back. Now.'

He gave him two fives, sent him striding off, hunched, hurrying away before the drive of cold, a knitted Rasta hat pulled about his ears. Hennessy watched him into the grey vanishing point, and then re-emergence, his smoky breath, until he was back.

'Jesus, man, cold out there!'

He flopped in his seat, filled himself with warm air, rubbed bleached palms like pistons, breathed on them.

'Your friend might be into pictures, maybe.'

'Photos?'

'On the wall, like, hard to see.'

'Camera?'

'Cameras black like spades, man!'

'People?'

'No people, faces, nothing.'

Hennessy nodded, waited, let him thaw in the hot spent air of the car, stretch his long springy legs a while.

'Someone up there maybe?'

'Open window. Could be, could be.'

'We'll sit a while.'

'Long while maybe, friend.' He smiled, leant close to Hennessy. 'You got a back-door pad there, man. Round the back, the garden gate.'

Hennessy nodded. 'Your parish,' he said.

'My home town, brother!'

'We'll go round soon.'

In the distance the first weak blur of fog was gathering: it would grow in icy smoke in a couple of hours, tighten its specks and ranks, lie and rub against tar and brick until morning paled it again. Now it sat soundless and cold on them; not even a wandering car broke the stillness of the road.

In half an hour Feehan, behatted, duffled, scarfed, shiny of shoe, appeared. He stood, a sentinel, a few moments on his steps. And then beside him a female, black close-cropped hair, tall; a figure of skirt and reefer, shoulder bag, flung-back scarf, long legs.

Feehan held open his car door for her; they drove into the growing blotch of the evening.

'Now,' Hennessy said. 'The garden gate.'

There had been gardens and gates once and high brick walls and stables facing each other across a service lane but dignity in retreat had burnt its bridges, scorched its earth: toppled brick-work and jungles of forgotten shrubbery had a smell of pro-phetic decay; street lights looked dimly distant at each other.

Hennessy had left the mini in wait, measured his walk, and squatted down in the piled dumped lumber of tenants past or dead or fled . . .

In a little while they came, Nally first, placid, even comfortable in the freezing air: a hard humourless face now, Hennessy thought, peering from the darkness. And then the fragile man, tall, unre-markable as sheepskin and thin mousy hair could make him. Nally said, 'Maida Vale. You could drop me there. I'll pick a car.'

They'd have rung for a cab, Hennessy knew, and suddenly the hard knock of the diesel was drawing close, probing into the darkness for them.

When they had gone stillness settled like a pond. Hennessy walked back to his minicab. Nally in a blacked-out room peeping at Feehan? At Feehan and guests? Or waiting for furniture? And the tall silent sheepskin? . . .

'My name is Rudi,' the minicab man said. They passed the old pile of St Mary's Hospital. 'I was born there like penicillin.' He gave Hennessy a gold-banded kingsize and flicked a lighter, lit what could have been a thin spill of pot for himself. His hands lay comfortable as sleeping cats on the steering wheel and he smiled out at the evening.

The crossroads at the Harrow and Edgware was a maelstrom and Marble Arch twinkled down the way.

'Archway first,' Hennessy said. 'Then Cricklewood.' He gave him another ten.

'Not fuzz bother, man?'

'Just careful,' Hennessy said.

'Right.'

The fog washed the whole darkening evening in dirty grey and convergence was losing ground; faces were clinched like fists against the cold.

'Camera back there, is it?'

'Maybe,' Hennessy said.

'Window up a crack! Take aim, fire, bang, bang!'

'That's it.'

'Someone taking pictures.' Rudi laughed softly, was pleased with the bizarre twist of the evening, pushed the money in a waistband fob. 'I like it. But no bombs, man, till I'm out of sight!' He almost lay on the steering wheel to brace himself against floods of amusement.

At an off-licence Hennessy bought whiskey and they pushed on to Euston and Islington and Highbury Corner and past the dying end of the Holloway Road.

'Funny,' Rudi said. 'You're the immigrant. Not me.'

'Bad enough being black,' Hennessy said.

His hands flopped against the dash to punctuate little pipes of laughter; he shook his head at the brilliance of it all.

From Archway Hennessy guided him in. 'Hold here,' he told him. 'I'll be a little while.'

Time had quickened its pace. Bleak fog and the wavering glint of tarmac slowed the whole pulse of the city; traffic crawled and spurted; café and pub windows were behind impenetrable steamy nets. He climbed the stairs, again travelled back along the endless day: the little laughing spitting man on the forecourt, Henderson, the polished brass, brave little Briggsie . . .

In Kirwan's room he groped in the rotting litter and felt the cord and still dry paper of his parcel. It was there. He smoothed back the ugly mound.

He opened the whiskey in his own room and there for a minute or two he sat in the darkness and drank a long burning mouthful. He shaved, dressed: a suit, shirt, tie, polished shoes and the warmth of the whiskey pushed back fatigue. He went down to the street again. It was a house of darkness: the centre floor condemned, boarded and sealed; Maisie at Cricklewood; even the basement caretaker, Kirwan's unbeloved, would be sipping her gin or stout or sweet barley wine in the blessed warmth and smoke of her boozer.

Rudi said, 'All that suit and stuff, brother!'

His eyes were full of sleepy peace and he nodded approval.

'Right?' Hennessy said; he gave him a ten.

'Cricklewood?'

Hennessy looked at his watch.

'Hurry, you said?'

'A little.' The fog was smoking, coming alive.

'You like music?' He snapped a cassette in its slot, swayed a little to the thump, drummed a finger now and then.

'OK?'

Hennessy nodded.

'Fog is on big now, man. Freezing too.'

Hennessy looked at patches of shiny road.

They went by Kentish Town now and Regent's Park and through Maida Vale and Kilburn. When Cricklewood loomed out of the grey, Hennessy said, 'This is it.'

'Take my card,' Rudi said. 'Any time, brother. Easy number, see? All threes, sixes, nines.' He moved away, still smiling, in a great throb of sound.

Hennessy, for a moment, looked at the blue and white card and dropped it in the frozen gutter. He could see the pub's suffusion of yellow light like an impressionist blob ahead. And then a few steps and he saw his truck at the kerb! Kirwan had arrived and only Kirwan, pissed, would leave a truck on the main drag within shout of a boozer! Christ, the parcel, Hennessy thought!

He moved past, scanned parked cars, pavements, doorways. But the fog was friend and enemy. Kirwan, wild, over the top? And had he lost Cleary, let him slip? . . .

56

He crossed the road to the pub forecourt, looked at the steaming, streaming windows; the thunder of voices and a lone thread of music belched and faded with each swing of the doors. He moved across the forecourt and pushed in . . .

From a phone box, in the middle distance, almost hidden, Nally watched him. His car was parked a little way off. He went to it and sat in the rear seat, hunched behind the storm collar of his Burberry. There was hardly fifteen minutes drinking left.

Another time Cleary, on his long tramp to Highbury, would have spotted the scarecrow drunken shadow of Kirwan. But the cold was unbearable. It stabbed deep into him so that even his mind seemed to shiver and he thought of Hennessy out on the six o'clock roads, the torture of early mornings, the greed it would take or the reward, to bolster against such hardship: the bare treads of Archway boarding houses and squats, the big twelve-wheeler dipped in filth, in hoar-frost. Jesus, you needed faith!

But who had shifted Hennessy's truck? There had been no nodding moment when Hennessy might have slipped him; the light had shone and been quenched in Hennessy's room but the truck had vanished and the little Greek mini driver had squealed like a pig hoisted by ear and tail . . .

Cleary stopped; his progress was almost a kind of weak trot. Coming down from Archway the gradient had pulled him along but on the flat of Seven Sisters Road the fog, as if the east wind stood still behind it, clung like an icy web. Had Hennessy clocked him, sent someone, the big gutted Kirwan maybe, to take the truck for an outing? Out of range. Money in the truck? Money in the house?

He would have pondered it but fear was growing. That moment, that once, he looked back but Kirwan, a hundred yards behind, smouldering, impatient in the long trudge, had stepped into an off-licence for whiskey, a flask for each pocket.

At Finsbury Park Cleary was jittery and even lickpenny greed faltered, but he tottered on, on home ground now, down to McLeod's imposing refuge. The glitter of frost was on the roads, a shadowy whiteness creeping along the roofs of parked cars. Beside him there were the random chequered lights in towering blocks of postwar flats skirting the main road and looking out over the broad stretch of Clissold Park: the fog distanced and froze in stillness the grassy mounds and trees.

It had been wealthy and staid and pretentious once, this hand-tailored seam of Stoke Newington and Highbury: but the elegance of London had always surged out from a brilliant core, leaving tide-marks of spent suburbs, a shabby grandeur as if the lights and music at a funfair had suddenly failed. The huge detached houses were let and sub-let, crammed like warrens. November, he thought, looking across at an open space where children had stockpiled the garnered junk and boxwood of a Guy Fawkes' bonfire.

He climbed the nine broad steps to McLeod's door, fumbled numbly with his key and even the faint warmth of the house was a flood of comfort. He lay back against the door: the hallway was chandeliered, carpeted, hung with canvases huge and minuscule, brass castings, a vast mirror anchored in a solid plaster tyre of gilt, old canes and walking sticks, a stylish half-moon table with old marble, a silver tray, everywhere the shiny skin of loving care.

Upstairs someone made a little whoop and pinned a tinkle of laughter to it and silence settled again. It was a house of men but McLeod's inversion had a Victorian dignity: his tenants were impeccable, their outrageous felicities sacrosanct as wells of loneliness and perfumed letters; even floor-to-floor promiscuity had a reserve of afternoon tea and calling-cards about it. McLeod's urges were sometimes sudden: Cleary had spotted him once in the small hours, naked and tight-fleshed, holding his sceptre like a flagpole, mounting the stairs for a swifty. But in fact McLeod was a vulgar bastard, coarse as crap. In the morning he had said, 'You had a squint last night, had you? Button up or I'll stuff you with a door-knob, that's a promise.' Cleary in his private solitary ecstasies felt clean, even wholesome, in contemplation of the encircling rot.

He had hardly begun to stir from his reverie when he heard

McLeod's taxi arrive: he didn't open the door for McLeod but walked a little way along the hall and waited. When McLeod appeared he said, 'Ah!'

McLeod said, 'Bastard night!'

'Fog. Freezing fog,' Cleary said. 'I'm just in.'

'I'll make coffee. Push on, push on!'

McLeod's harsh patronage sent out little prods of resentment: he disliked McLeod's coffee, it was thick and bitter, needing somehow to be different. He would have told him to push it but there was a free room, bed and board, run of the larder, little bunces here and there, fares in the elastic line of duty: a solid bedrock economy. The pay envelopes from Bredin need scarcely be touched. He thought a little bleakly about it: at the outset, fifty clear on a Friday was the escalator to wealth, a place, independence. In three years he had over seven thousand – but the future was in flight, it seemed, the goal more distant than ever. He looked at the comfort of McLeod's mansion, thought of the rents, thought of money in Hennessy's truck. Hennessy's doss? It was like a screwing gimlet of pain.

McLeod's living-room was raw: that was the inadequate word that sprang always to Cleary's mind when he entered. It was a spacious three-roomed basement with a kind of conservatory and steps mounting to a walled garden with grass, shrubs, trees, a sunhouse. But it was raw and skinless, the floor boards bare and scrubbed white, the furniture, even a small old fashioned wireless set, were without paint or varnish; the walls and ceiling brilliant white plaster; the element of the light bulb shone out nakedly, giving a comfortless light. There were no books or newspapers or ashtrays or pictures or photographs to relieve the austerity. It was the kind of elaborate joke that McLeod wouldn't need to share with anyone.

Cleary looked at the telephone, numberless, special: it was black and shining and extraordinarily elegant. There was a telephone at McLeod's bedside too, numbered, listed, as ordinary as red could make it.

McLeod came with white mugs of coffee; the coffee was black; he wore a brown dustcoat, hanging open, like a checker or a shopman from long ago.

'You weren't at Paddington tonight,' he said.

'No.'

'I didn't see you.'

Cleary thought about that. 'I scouted round.'

'Ah?'

'Sometimes there's a straw in the wind and I chase it.'

'Yes?'

'Straws come to ground.'

'Anything?'

'Dead-end.'

'Local, was it?'

'A pub. West Hampstead,' Cleary lied.

'Bring your coffee,' McLeod said; he had soft yellow buffers in each pocket and be brought a feather brush from the kitchen. 'We'll do some dusting.'

Christ! Cleary thought; he plodded behind him, remembering the sounds McLeod made in the kitchen: the opening and shutting of things, the tinkle of ware, a single line from a tune he kept repeating. Sweet and sour in Cleary's ears. He would have a place like this one day and mope about at midnight or later and have a warm bedroom and get up in the quietness of mid-morning when the whole world was in a sweat . . .

He climbed the stairs to the hallway and entered McLeod's 'drawing room': a brass plaque declaring 'Private' hung from the door-knob.

'You went to Paddington then?' Cleary said.

McLeod pitched a yellow cloth at him. 'Get your hands off your nuts. Makes you round-shouldered. Yes, I went to Paddington.'

'Anything special?'

'Just a tip-off. Let me finish this elephant of rosewood.' He began to dust an immense grand piano; a candelabrum of white filigreed silver stood on it, half-burned candles, keys exposed, music on the rack.

'A traveller?' Cleary asked.

'Truck driver. Walworth somewhere. In Archway too. Give him a whirl. Forget Paddington a while.'

'Important?'

'Oh, I don't know.' He brushed it aside, sounded a chord or two, made his perennial grinning jokes. 'Sexy jiggy little things had their arses here, you know, sweaty drawers too, singing love and stainless passion, ravenous little bitches.' He flicked the feather brush along the tapestry of the piano stool. 'Let the odd fart too, I suppose.' He looked at Cleary's distaste. 'Observers can be observed, you see, when the game is clever,' he said suddenly. 'Paddington.'

'He was due at Feehan's, was he?' Cleary said. 'This driver?'

'Oh yes . . . keep working for Christ's sake, we don't want to spend the night! . . . the bastard didn't show.' McLeod with his feather brush was dusting gilt frames, strange blackened canvases. It was an enormous room, cluttered with enormous furniture, paintings and bric-à-brac and it had the brilliant tenuous health of an old bed-ridden person waiting for death; there should have been layers of dust and the smell of stale mildewed air and a sadness in the vulgarity of everything. But the room was alive: an instant ago people of another age might have passed them in the doorway. ' . . . Get a bit of steam up, laddie!'

Bollicks, Cleary thought.

McLeod stopped for a moment. 'A taxi passed through. It isn't a usual route for taxis.'

'No,' Cleary said.

'He could be clever, you see?'

'Yes.'

Except for the faint touch of dusters the silence was complete. Legs, dowels, panels, finials, door frames, window frames, glass, porcelain, metal. It was turned half past ten.

'We'll call a halt now,' McLeod said but he went on dusting and tidying: the chandelier swayed gently and trembled like something huge and poisonous in a deep-sea pool; it made a dull tinkling noise; vases stood on mahogany pedestals; there was a lovers' chair, a rosewood cabinet of china miniatures and glass and automata; the tapestry curtains, a little faded, were shrouding stained-glass door to a kind of cloistered loggia. And beyond it, the walled garden.

'Right, that's it!' McLeod said; he appraised it all for a

moment. 'Hennessy might be his name, I think. Ring a bell?'

'There are a lot of drivers,' Cleary said. 'They come and go.'

'Keep an eye.'

'Yes.'

'Coffee?'

'No,' Cleary said. 'I'll pack it.' He raised his hand as he went upstairs to his room.

McLeod said 'Good night', and went down to his skinless lounge. At eleven the telephone in his bedroom rang and Nally said, 'He's here. Cricklewood. I'll stay with it a while.'

'Our mutual archivist,' McLeod said.

'Cleary?'

'Playing games I think. Never heard of Hennessy. Not sure at any rate.'

After ten or fifteen seconds Nally said, 'I'll be in touch.'

In his bedroom Cleary, in growing warmth, deep exquisite satisfaction, heard the faint ring of the telephone before he drifted away. He had thought of the taxi, the tip-off; Hennessy with McLeod only fresh on his tail. The warmth had cushioned and brushed away fear: he was ahead of them all.

There was an outside john at the Cricklewood pub, a kind of relief office opened at night-time only to take the tide of overspill when inside loos were crammed and inadequate. In the freezing air steam billowed out and was swallowed in the fog. Hennessy could get the sharp tang of urine. He moved away from it towards the bar entrance, scanned the forecourt, its cars, its vans. It was a night of hunched hurried movements, not for lingering. He saw the edge of a phone box showing in the distance, a figure there, pondered it a moment and dismissed it.

The pub's hot reeking air was a fabric, a cling-film; it enveloped him: a thunder of shuffle and voice, instant laughter sometimes shrill as a scream; faces hung on a whole smoky canvas for Brueghel or Munch or Bosch, and the music was a projectile hurled down from mounted speakers in a hopeless battle of decibels, a drowning noise perhaps noticed in its absence.

The raised stage seemed small and distant in the smoke, painted over in a grey imperfect glaze; and there was Maisie, a white blob of face and frantic elbow. In the turmoil her smart dress, tight blonde curls, were a needless extravagance. It was her moment of the evening, standing centre-mike, her jigs and reels hardly penetrating the first skin of crashing sound.

Hennessy pushed through the crowd; a slow progress. The counter ran end to end, sixty, seventy feet of it, staff arranged, deployed like men-at-arms on the ramparts.

He saw Feehan first: the brushed grey velour hat, its indigo band, the wedge face of an outrageous savage gargoyle. And the girl beside him. There was a bleak smile of caution in her face, a tightness of lip.

Then closer, it loomed suddenly before him, the flaming red mask of Kirwan, drunk, helpless, spoiling for Armageddon. On the counter he had put a fistful of change, a pack of kingsize, the keys of the truck. There was no drink. Staff passed, ignored him, with a hurrying effortless professionalism. A minder, remote as a saint, hovered not far away.

'A drink for Christ's sake!' The noise, the smoke, diminished, obliterated him; he held the counter with one hand, made a fist with the other and hammered. 'A drink! And a drink for the fiddle player!'

Maisie had played the last of her screaming notes and gave a show-biz smile from her seat; if there had been applause it had been sucked into the turbine of roar and babble.

Feehan raised a hand for service, was smiled on at once. 'Mr Feehan?' She was stout, flat-faced, an androgynous pile who might spit on her hands and swing a pick-axe; but she was aware of rank, importance. 'Three halves of malt, Mr Feehan? And for the lady? Martini dry, ice and slice?'

Feehan nodded; behind him a couple of lieutenants stood, mean, beer-gutted, tough.

Kirwan was close to his peace, flushed with a deep burning glow that spread down to his neck, shaping soundless words with lips and brown greasy teeth.

'Coming up, Mr Feehan!' The great ponderous woman beamed.

'Mister Bollicks!' Kirwan roared in sudden restoration of speech and they stood shocked around a little private pool of silence as at a burial.

The lieutenants stirred but Feehan brought them to heel.

'You belong down a hole, a big big hole, mister-me-friend,' he said to Kirwan. With a beer mat he carefully gathered up Kirwan's change, keys, fags, drew them to the edge of the counter, let them topple over.

Kirwan's rage was a sudden bloody percussion in his mind and for a moment power drained away and he was groping at air, swaying, gommy, loose-jawed.

'Pick up your rubbish and move,' Feehan told him.

Kirwan was a flat rubber shape, inflating; a lifeless arm was filled, suddenly quivered and snapped to rigidity. Whiskies, vermouth, ice and slice rushed at Feehan, his tie, the executive duffel; the flies of his suit darkened and he could feel the cold alcohol at his crotch; liquor droplets, broken glass, speckled his shoes. The girl beside him was wary in an instant, tight as a spring.

Kirwan said in a fierce whisper, a triumphant snarl of gums and teeth, 'You'll find men down the holes, on their feet, on their backs! Men! Not dressed-up fucking goats, second-hand generals! A sniff of the gelly you'd be gone for the trots with wet on your leg . . . you bastard!'

Hennessy was beyond the range of voices but across shoulders he could see the pallor that slapped against Feehan's face, as if a world had crumbled, the drop of his jaw, eyes fixed like a startled ferret. Kirwan grew bigger. The minders stirred and settled. The girl searched for escape, a cleft in the crowd where she could lodge, vanish. It was a jungle.

Hennessy fought through the last yards of sweat and flesh, was held tight, then spun at the counter between them.

Feehan said, 'Out!' No movement, only a measuring glance at Hennessy, a dismissal of him.

'I thought we might talk furniture,' Hennessy said to draw him off. 'But you picked a bad night for it. Mister.'

'Move, I told you!'

For Kirwan, out of the swirl of fading senses, the picture

64

stilled and sharpened for a moment. 'Hennessy!' he roared in a long rising moan of victory and battle-cry. He gripped Hennessy's shoulders. 'See the mongrel dogs that get in a decent field! See! Frothing dangerous bastards!' He was in the last delirious moments before peace and darkness.

Searching for forgiveness in Feehan's face, or even pity, was a barren journey; a smile or a headshake to him wouldn't find understanding or dull the edge of savagery.

'Move, mister!' he told Hennessy. 'Or get your teeth rattled. Suit yourself.' The huge fist was hoisted slowly, menacing as a jib. And suddenly Kirwan loomed and was blundering at him, words, dangerous, jumbled, rising to a barrack-room shout. And they stung.

Feehan had been crouched to strike and he froze in an instant, movement ceased like a power-cut, shock imploded and fear and doubt. He seemed to wait for a thousand cracks that would rend him asunder. Kirwan tottering towards him became a shadow almost beyond consciousness, only the incredible catapulted words were of importance. He side-stepped and let him blunder into the crowd. His thin goat's face tilted and gaped. For a moment the music struggled to life, was audible, and then just as instantly lost. Kirwan was rushing for battle again and Hennessy tripped him, sent him sprawling out of danger between stools and the counter. He lost sight of Feehan for an instant and felt the stony fist thump against his forehead and was blind with pain. In two, three, seconds the crowd would close, moments for the minders and boots, whatever could bludgeon; confusion everywhere; Feehan would be masked out of sight, out of range, and Hennessy needed to feel the deadening numbness of his own hand when he shattered him. He saw him for an instant lunging in attack again, the fist drawn back like a sledge to shatter everything before it, and he leant forward, a jerk of hips and shoulder and forearm, to meet the oncoming face, felt it lifted, driven away before the savage force of the blow. He followed him, dragging himself through the crowd until he found him thrown back against the counter, still dazed, holding his huge palms like shutters across his face. He hit him below the ribs and again in the face as he doubled, and fell with him to the floor. And there lay Kirwan in a forest of legs, oblivious, beyond pain, his money, the fags, the truck keys scattered about him. Hennessy picked the keys. The girl's legs were beside him swaying in a tumble-dance with the crowd. Feehan, hatless, showing a pale tonsure, was on his knees in vomit. And overhead, up on the surface of the storm, the lounge was in uproar. Touched-off scuffles, battles, flared like pre-conceived diversions. The music died instrument by instrument, note by note. Hennessy grabbed at the girl's stockinged knees and pulled himself to his feet. The whirring of squad cars jittered the forecourt, spotlights flung a glare of yellow dye on the windows.

'Law!' Hennessy shouted in her ear; he hardly saw the pale face, eyes glittering, hard as stone.

The doors were jammed in a syphon of bodies aimed at the forecourt but he grabbed her wrist, reached the counter, lifted her as she jumped, put her beyond the reach of a minder, an ageing bull beginning his charge. Hennessy vaulted, watching him, dug feet in the softness of belly as he landed.

Behind, a kind of back-stage, was a choked passage of kegs, piled crates, an exit and beyond it a laneway mews. They reached it. A single pilot light heightened the gloom: dustbins, refuse, a few parked bangers; a big shape and glinting buttons, the scrape of feet coming for them, a torchlight jerking like a drunken follow-spot. They were in the lee of a battered van.

'Against the door,' she said. She pulled Hennessy in to her, encircled him with her arms, kissed him with a mouthing wriggling passion.

The follow-spot danced, wandered, returned, until it reached their welded faces.

'What's on?' the Law said.

'Just a chat,' Hennessy told him.

'More like a fucking dog-fight.' He shone the torch on Hennessy's flies, the girl's skirt.

'We are kissing too,' she said. 'Doing everything. We love each other you see.' She had found an accent now and made a slow deliberate choice of words; her fingers held Hennessy's arm tight as a clamp. 'You, I hope, don't mind.'

The Law said, with a sour trace of humour, 'Learning English, are we?' and gazed po-faced at her happiness. 'Micks have big big pricks, give you a little packet for Momma in gay Paree. Move off!' He looked long and hard at Hennessy.

They went out into the glare of the forecourt; Marias were zooming in. It was a sea of vehicles. In one, Nally might have been a sleeping drunk in the back seat, hidden down behind his collar. The fog was thickening, floating like grey smoke in the flood-beams. It was cold as a slab.

'I have a truck,' Hennessy said. 'I'll put you down somewhere.'

She remained silent, linked him; they walked on the pavements, leaving the forecourt, the whirring fuzz behind them. She was close and randy.

'Don't get any ideas,' she said. 'This little show's for the Law. They sit like micks in their motors, bright as buttons, radios even, mod cons you never dreamed of. Or did you?'

'I don't have much time,' Hennessy said. 'This is it. The truck.'

She was suddenly loose, swinging away, but Hennessy grabbed her before she turned, slapped down the knee shooting for his groin. He held her close at the waist, with a fistful of tight hair tilted her face towards him.

'You're in bother, you stupid bastard!' she said. 'I can smell it. On the trot. Not for me. I'm out!'

'You're in,' Hennessy said. 'Believe it. You're in.'

They stood close, in silence, like lovers, while a whole minute crawled past. Hennessy's hands slowly released her. 'I have a villain on my tail, that's all,' he said. 'Another kind of dog eat dog. But for you, it's time to move. Believe it.' He opened the truck door. There was no parcel in the driver's seat and he hoped Kirwan had left it at Maisie's, or could even remember. Dear Christ, he thought . . .

The girl climbed in. 'Where?'

'Not far,' he told her. 'A few minutes. In fog a little longer.'

She sat partly against the door, to face him, the bulky leather shoulder-bag on her knees: she was herself now, the words were rolled spears of steel snipped instant by instant and launched speeding towards a target. 'I have this,' she said: it was a gun. 'When I call a halt I'll mean it.'

'Save it,' he said. 'You might need it soon.' The truck struggled, shuddered to life, the dims made shallow incandescent burrows in the fog. At fifty yards it was a solid grey wall; the wipers, slow, gathered the filthy ooze on the windscreen.

Travelling in fog was moving in a slow weeping capsule through space where even sound was distanced. He felt the tight throbbing mound on his forehead where Feehan had struck, thought a moment of Kirwan stretched in drunken peace and Feehan's vomit in a pool about his knees; Cleary peering about at Archway. Had Kirwan lost him? Was the small man at Edmonton coughing gobs of phlegm in the fog and waiting for cowboys; or Henderson in his red room, fireworks forgotten? Eighty-four thousand . . .

He saw that Feehan's blood was spread along his knuckles, his hand, his wrist. Where was Nally? The absence of Nally had a guerrilla's craft in it. He looked in his mirror: only yellow blobs in the smoke; and ahead, red tail-lights tired of squinting. For a moment only he remembered the distant phone box at Cricklewood . . .

He had pushed down through Kilburn and Maida Vale, knowing every turn and kerb, and was moving in for Paddington now.

'Where are we?' the girl said.

He looked across at her shoes, moving, tapping; the ankles, stockinged legs, knees, the skirt hem, the shoulder-bag. He could feel her distaste.

'Where are we?'

'Not long now.'

'Christ!'

'Paddington,' he said.

'This?'

'Paddington, Paree, Bogside, brick walls, Holloway Gates, fog paints them all.'

. . . He pulled into the kerb by the entrance to McLeod's service road and in an instant she was on the pavement, the shoulder bag in front, both hands deep in it as if for warmth. Hennessy walked round and nodded at the almost black mouth

68

of the alleyway. There was only silence and the street lights barely glowing.

She saw a heavy steel pinch-bar in Hennessy's hand. 'What's on?'

'Important for me. For you too,' Hennessy said; he moved into the darkness and crumbling walls, the ghostly shadows of gardens gone wild; he could hear her following.

'Why?'

'Save your breath.'

He found McLeod's entrance, the iron stairway, the studio door. He waited until she had climbed the steps and was beside him and thought of Nally again and listened, peered at nothingness.

'This is a fox-hole,' he said. He pushed the flat wedge-end of the pinch-bar between door and jamb, leant against it until the creaking strain mounted to crackle and split. There was a tiny foyer that had once been a landing, and a single door led to McLeod's belvedere. It was open, the curtains drawn, hardly a glimmer of light filtering from the shrouded street lamps. Hennessy found the table light and let its paleness slowly bring substance to the shadow.

Cameras, prints, blow-ups, posters, old streets, young bodies, faded carpet, glasses, the heavy smell of brandy. She stood in the doorway and he watched her examine it with slow expressionless progress. It struck him that he hadn't seen her stand apart before: she had been knees or passionless eyes or lips of wet and slop, ankles, stockinged legs, even a voice toneless as tannoy-snap. But she was tall, stylish even, and the hardness at close quarters was, at distance, reserve. The dark cropped hair was tight as a puritan cap.

'You could call it the stake-out,' he said. With the pinch-bar he smashed hollow cameras and tripods. 'Dummies, phonies,' he said. 'But not this one.'

She came across to stand behind and stare down at the low-perched Nikon aimed for the street. Hennessy shattered light and table lamp with a single flail, held back a wedge of curtain. She was looking across at the door, the granite treads to Feehan's flat. He watched the slow stepping-stones of recognition, the

69

quickening, the pause, the quickening, the final cautious reassessment of everything: a lidless dustbin, the door number, its colour, window curtains ... the camera.

She nodded, without emotion: no shock, fear, puzzlement, gratitude. 'Feehan.'

Hennessy let the curtains swing tight, smashed the Nikon. It was empty. 'Feehan is a tool, a gull, that's all, for Christ's sake!'

They went down through the black tunnel of jungle alleyway. The cab of the truck had almost a warmth after the gripping chill of frost and fog. Hennessy drove into what minutes were left before midnight, towards Marylebone and Euston. A long day.

'Where?'

'Place to place. Moving, just moving,' he said.

'Feehan?'

'He'll be tidied up with the rest when it's time.'

'There's a house in Woolwich,' she said: she recited the number, the road.

At Bermondsey the River loops again about the Isle of Dogs, touching Deptford and Greenwich, and then in a wider arc moves on through East Ham and Barking Level towards the broader reaches: a slow powerful stream looking out at the extreme ugliness of its road. From Tooley Street at London Bridge there is nothing but grime and ageing masonry and streets that never had grace; the tunnels beneath the River leave the tails of their traffic sprawling across the inadequate thoroughfares and the houses are small, made to face each other across narrow spaces.

By the River it would always be a thickening fog, sucking in the darkness of mud and marsh, oil-spills, forgotten dying wharves and jetties; and it was the time of day when tiredness overtook him without warning. You were burnt out, unaware of it: a body grew sluggish like an overheated piston, the stomach swelled out against the tightness of muscles. His head and shoulders ached with leaning forward to squint at footways.

Now ground sweat was rising and the houses, dim shop windows, seemed to retire behind it, to throb away remotely in another life beyond the noise of slowed-down traffic and gliding wing-lights like candles floating on a stream.

In half an hour he tired of the inch and creep of traffic. Fog, like a layer of sleep, muffed the windows and windscreen, the wiper motor pulled him into its monotony; sometimes he put a hand in pocket for rest. Suddenly he turned into the side-streets: a vacant lot, a desolate junction of stone-paved alleys almost in darkness with the imprisoned fog. The lights of somewhere glimmered from far across space, but peace was there, as if only the last all-rending explosion, decades ago, that had created it, was the maker of hush and tranquillity. He stood on the humped scabrous ground, watched, listened. The girl climbed carefully down from the cab.

'Is there someone?'

'I don't know.'

'For you, for me?'

'The Law for you, a Big Man's minders for me, who knows? Or only ghosts, maybe.' In a little while he said, 'Your name isn't important, I suppose?'

'No.'

He nodded, turned away to close his eyes in weariness; his head ached where Feehan had landed; he could feel the tightness of skin. He rested a while in the bombed-out stillness. It was past midnight but children with mugs and a guy came out of the fog and passed close by and in a few paces had vanished like fragments of thoughts; time gathered and fell with the steady drip of wetness from the belly of the truck.

'You know it?'

'I know the road,' Hennessy said.

'A café.'

'Caffs aren't hard to find.'

He drove back to the High Road, to the snail of traffic, and turned for Woolwich. The whole sourness of a winter's day must tap and throb behind a metronome infinity of wiper blades; two men, fat comic revenants in the fog, stood by the locked fenders of their cars, a careful one writing in his notebook, the other dejectedly staring out into the greyness for the sympathy of mankind. Someone along the line hooted him and he trembled and swore and might even have wept. He was the impatience of the whole world ...

Hennessy probed along the vanished road, where had been the Arsenal walls and inside the bleak acres swept away: the factories and stores and scrap dumps, and the smell of obsolescence hung down like the fog: they were gone, might never have been.

He had known clear sweet air once, he tried to remember: a whole sky, a warm day, the chill of wind and tide. He remembered it always in clear patches of sky or tawny summer mornings when he drove muck loads down by the awakening parks. But it too was gone ...

The house came up out of the smoke. She pointed. Hennessy had seen it on a laneway corner: a transport caff, peeling paint, netted windows, no glimmer of light.

He turned into the laneway, fitted tightly between slivers of pavement. There was a side-door only feet ahead.

He watched her ring the bell, stand waiting, a hand deep down finding warmth in the shoulder-bag. She was already smiling: he could see the tilt of her chin, the crease of jaw. The door opened on a six-inch chain and a face hovered. In a few moments she moved inside, beckoned Hennessy as she went.

He locked the truck, stepped into the total blackout of the hallway. The walls were painted black, a black weighted curtain hung at the end. The girl was gone.

'Come, darling.' There was a floating mask, fluttering hands in the darkness, magic like puppetry. He could hear voices faintly, smell tobacco and the comforting mix of booze. But she left him in the empty caff: tables, chairs, plastic, metal; beyond the net curtains the candle-light traffic, funeral of the unholy, crept past.

'Wait,' she said, strangely tender and comforting: the make-up might crack and fall away like dry plaster. 'And no smoking, darling.' She nodded at the visible world outside, stood for a moment, wasted, fragile, and left him.

Come, sit, wait. He might growl or bark another time but this was shelter and he needed breathing space. A lifetime's loot in Maisie's sitter, and under Kirwan's creeping pile. Nally on his tail. The camera man? He wiped the blood from his hand with spittle. He knew now there might be no parley: all or nothing. Nally, alone, was a match maybe; Nally, in alliance, and it was time to run.

... An old man if ever you see Camden Town again, he remembered.

He looked about at the dim pin-ups and nudes stuck haphazardly on the walls, a vast gallery of them, a wealth of unattainable desire, twisted, arranged, shadowed, flooded, poised, aimed: the magnificent defenceless country postured before the enemy, everything exposed, even the weapons. The corners of the room shrunk away from the gloom. There was a counter at the end with crescents and diamonds painted on it, a tea urn, a glass case guarding a single cheese roll; a heavy brown curtain on brass rings swayed a little as if there might be an opening to a kitchen. There was no untidiness or litter but somehow the room was dirty. The tea, he thought, would be unpleasant as if sickness had been slowly brewed in it ...

When the voice chimed out again it was like a call from off-stage, a gay mannered accent dipped for an instant in refinement. 'Darling.' The face might be a chalky cast, spectral, on a drape.

He followed her beyond the curtain: there was a journey by passageways to a door.

'Come, come!'

And then a large space, a function-room of an old boozer, maybe. At the open fire, small settees facing each other, a telephone, a lamp. On the floor, a square marked out in white heavy tape, an apron; church pews, two rows, framed it. A little theatre. Amber light flooded down from the ceiling, in warmth, in expectancy. In daylight, with ashes in a cold grate and greyness falling on the nudity of everything, it would have a spent ugliness.

'Sit down, sit down, darling.' She came in behind him, sat close to the fire, the lamp, the phone. 'The settee, love. Sit facing me. That's nice. Push things out of your way.'

The settees were littered with old discarded newspapers and mags that had been lain on often and shaped over the bulging contours of the seat. The light shone on her face now and he could see the yellow streaks of unwashed make-up ebbing back to her scalp; her eyes were clear and healthy. She might be sixty; older perhaps.

'Always fog down here,' she said, 'the River, dirt, sewers, all that shit.'

She was smiling at him; and beyond the door, the passage-ways, the net curtains, the traffic was a small remote disturb-ance. Voices, smoke, the noise of glasses, were nearer. Her smile was pleasant and adequate as the off-stage sing-song voice.

'I like the fog,' she said, expecting that he should wonder and be amused.

'Yes?'

'Hides everything.'

'The only house in space.'

'The only room,' she said, laughing and almost proud of him. 'Some nights I sleep here.'

'Feet up, look at the fire, listen to the foghorns on the River.'

She was pleased, disarming, missed nothing; she looked at his skinned knuckles. 'Gave yourself a right old knock on the nut, didn't you? What about a drink, Pat?' She opened the door of what might have been a bedside locker and he saw the bottles stacked inside. 'I'm selling it, love. Can't afford to give it away.'

'How much?'

'Ten nicker the half-bottle to you. Cheap. Should be a score.' She poured two whiskies.

'I'm buying yours too?' Hennessy said.

She made a saucy childish face: unspeakable. 'For Paddy in the parlour with a bottle you're the cagey one, eh?' She drank the liquor back. 'I won't be long, love. If someone comes, you're a friend of Sadie's.'

When she had gone he could hear the flat rambling morse of the fire, the shift of coals, fog signals braying down on the River. A strange easeful hearth. He thought of Kirwan clatter-ing out from the bleak rooms, fleeing with a five or a ten or a

74

twenty to his own refuge of numbness. And Nally, Feehan, Cleary, the girl? Hennessy? Old crones in corners with beads and certainties had the edge.

Sadie had gone out a side-door and when it opened again now, voices and laughter were immediately there, someone calling from upstairs, sounds of a warm embracing house, of comings and goings. A coloured man came in, a pleasant blend of Arab and Afro in his face; he said, 'Hello, old man, foggy night out there, what?' Very sure of himself. Two blonde girls followed him. He introduced them like an off-hand magician, proud yet humble with his trick. 'Friends of mine. Damn fog is lousy, what? Play yourselves some music, girls. My friend won't mind.'

He was tall; and good-looking when the big lips parted and his teeth shone; his clothes were pale grey and elegant, almost draining away the excess of rings and cufflinks, wrist-chains, gold washed writing pens. He took glasses from Sadie's locker, poured Hennessy's whiskey. 'We will have a drink with you, what? Very sociable!' He smiled. 'Have a drink, girls. On my good friend here.'

Music had swirled out from a cassette hidden somewhere behind the accumulated junk of Sadie's corner; the girls switched to ecstatic motion; long leisurely appraisals of their thighs and buttocks as they spun and jerked in the magic apron.

'Good?' he said; it might have been the whiskey or the thighs.

Hennessy watched: knees together, hips wagging; knees apart, backs arched, heads thrown back, mouths a little open; the whang whang beat of the music.

'Sadie tells me you're a Paddy, likes you too. No worries, Pat.' He came close. 'I'm Somali. African, you see. Not bloody Carib! African!'

Hennessy watched him seeming to smile at something tenderly pleasant in the fire. The room and its chattels were no longer remarkable; it had been a dead stage awaiting its players.

'A friend of Sadie's?'

'He is.' She drifted across before them to her place. 'An old friend.' She had forced her thin boniness into tight calf-length britches, like a matador's, and a woollen sweater showed her flat as a board; she was like a corpse revived, suddenly charged with an excess of energy; her eyes were clear and brilliant with a sniff or a shot behind them. 'A bag of old bones, ain't I, Paddy?' she said. 'Stand me a drink, I'll show you me navel, stand me two and I won't.'

The Somali laughed now and in his laughter he seemed to slump like a discarded marionette; but he was watchful; he might have owned Sadie and the house and the little go-gos. There were more than a dozen people in the room now, a gathering crowd, finding pews or standing at the walls; the girls brought drinks from the hallway or beyond; the thump of beat music and the sound of people in excitement throbbed in space. The Somali still laughed and shrugged.

Sadie said, 'Drink some whiskey, love.' She passed him the lees of his bottle. It was a dreamy isolated voice as if she were still in the one silent room in space, listening to the sounds of the fire and fog sirens out on the River. Only her eyes were alive. 'And here's your girl,' she whispered. 'Likes to dress up, don't she? Ain't she a doll?'

Hennessy saw the tall raunchy blonde come at him: lank streaked hair, the botch of make-up; crude; leather skirt, black, taut, high as a mini; shimmering grey tights, ankle-straps, a red roll-neck sweater, painted nails, a bangle, a gaudy metal chain at her neck.

Sadie grinned. 'Look at them bristols, Pat! Could sleep there, couldn't you? And legs go all the way up.'

Hennessy looked: the eyes hadn't changed, he thought.

'We'll call her Kiki, eh? I'd a mouser once called Kiki. Make room for Kiki.'

Jesus, Hennessy thought.

She had arsed in beside him; the crossing of legs was a crackle of static; the reek of scent poisoned him.

'Hello, Pat,' she said. 'How's your luck?'

The voice, the chiselled words were real. He looked from the slap-dash mouth to the grey expressionless eyes behind pencil and shadow. Her face was close to his. 'Call me Kiki, love. I don't need bother, remember?'

Sadie was nodding.

'All you need is a hunting knife,' Hennessy said.

She smiled with everything except her eyes, put a little kiss on his cheek. 'And don't get any ideas, Pat.'

Hennessy tired of it.

The crowd moved, was restless like a scummy corner of a dock-basin, never erupting, but heaving and oily; people were there and gone and suddenly appearing again; there were always new girls and drinks and laughter and a hammering impatience in the room. The Somali watched as if absences might be of some immense importance.

It was a timeless place, suspended neither in darkness nor in light, and its chaos and dilapidations might have been a studied expensive gimmick. Sadie had begun to move about, to mingle, a kind of Chelsea fringe long-playing hostess, burdened with charm. He could hear her laughing beyond the noise and music, see her hands fluttering like birds.

'That your truck in the alley?' the Somali said.

Hennessy nodded.

'Nearly bashed the old banger on it. Damn fog. Can't see a bloody thing. The girls screamed.' He laughed, remembering it, glanced expertly at Kiki. 'Truck driver. Tough job.'

'Very.' Hennessy said, and watched him glide into the evening.

The lights dimmed except for the centre flood; excitement stirred in the dark plumes of the room, like a rustle of flimsy clothes; the fog horns boomed on the River, lost baleful cattle wandering in greyness. Sadie returned to sit, with fag and glass, poised at the fire. The cassette jolted to silence. In the taped apron of floor the Somali bowed and smiled, told with great charm old predictable jokes and his teeth shone like toilet slabs. He backed gracefully away from the applause, clapped his hands for silence, stood behind Hennessy and the girl. 'This is good,' he said to Hennessy; and then remembered to add, 'It costs you nothing. Free. I lay it on for my customers.' Sadie was watching him. 'Sadie engages me, you see?'

She acknowledged his submission.

A passage had been left from the side-door. There was an off-stage clash of cymbals. A couple raced on, two men, not young, not old, in drag, prancing, smiling such weary smiles, Hennessy thought: smiles out of some echoing chamber of laughter and derision. They brought a folding table and chairs and sat in the taped arena to play at pout and strip; the dialogue was a spitting match of obscenities exciting laughter and applause, the humour excremental, thickly buttered on a reechy slice of wasting time. Little snapping sounds, stockings rolled away from flesh, things unbuttoned, everything slow, almost reluctant. Another game, a moue of shock, beleaguered modesty, applause jittering in the room, a breathlessness. And then with unexpected speed one was naked, dancing about, sitting on knees, offering his powdered arse like a bon-bon to have beer sprinkled on it, a slice of lemon, a puff of smoke. Applause followed him on his lap of honour. Then they were together again, embracing, shunting: one slid down the other's body, kissing it inch by inch, taking wispy briefs with him. A stout impressive dildo was unveiled, erect as a stanchion. Then, dog and dog, they were coupling.

The Somali whispered to Hennessy, 'The real thing, you see, not simulated! The real thing, it goes in, you see it?'

In a few moments it was consummated, they smiled their deathly smiles, the flood faded, they were gone. The cassette boomed out, light was a sudden glare, the crowd flowed back into the pool . . .

Hennessy thought of night-time outside, the real or unreal world, streets in stillness now, traffic gone. And Nally? Was he out there, patient as justice? Or in Highgate, in a bastion built about his comfort, resting for the last day's battle that would soon be a pale streak in the sky. He could have beaten Nally. But Nally and the sheepskin and pictures? It should be time to run.

Sadie said to him softly, 'You didn't like that, Pat? I can tell, you know. A bit filthy, wasn't it? But it pays the rent, love. That's the bottom line, ain't it.'

He nodded, handed her a twenty. 'Another half. The extra ten's for Christmas.'

'You're a good lad, Pat,' she said. 'I hope Kiki loves you.'

'Madly,' Kiki said.

Hennessy put the whiskey in his pocket. 'Is there another phone?' he asked.

Sadie nodded.

'Coin-box in the hall,' the Somali told him; he was thoughtful; he moved away, collecting the props of the entertainers, accepted slaps and congratulations as if on impulse he had manufactured passion to pass for them the small foggy hours of the morning. His friends crowded him with talk but when Hennessy passed he was back with Sadie.

'Who is this bastard friend of yours?' he asked. 'And this randy piece of tail he pulled?'

'Watch your blown-up lips, Sambo!' she told him; she had a little slender wine glass in her hand that would splinter into thin needles of glass.

'Who is he?'

'You'll excuse him pet, won't you?' she said to Kiki.

'He sees my show!' the Somali said. 'He sees my show, he on the phone! I have to use my brains, see?'

'Your brains are down too low, love. Go on, piss off!'

She picked up the phone beside her, listened to Hennessy's number ringing. In a few seconds an ansafone intoned 'Mercer House, Highgate' and Hennessy was saying, 'Archway. Top of the house, on the left. Yours under the pile. That's quits.' He repeated it, hung up.

'Yes?' the girl said.

Sadie spoke it aloud for her. 'Highgate ansafone. All right, is it?'

'Archway, top of the house?'

'On the left . . . yours under the pile . . . that's quits. Means something, does it?'

'Yes.'

Hennessy pushed back through the crowd; he had rung Nally; the Somali smiled and waved. The morning hours were getting bigger. At the fire he said to the girl, 'We should take a walk, Kiki, talk a little. All right, Sadie?'

'Course,' she said. 'Another strip, we're shut at five. And Pat, mind how you go?' She brought a black beret, a red tie-belt coat for the girl, arranged things, patted the shoulder-bag, took

79

them through the black hallway, graciously shut them out.

The fog was lifting a little but it was still a grey wandering smoke catching the vapour of breath, ice cold. The roads and pavements were bright as varnish.

'You wanted to talk,' the girl said. 'A little.'

'Soon.'

Hennessy took the deserted side-streets, almost untenanted, old as dockers' carts, cobbles, dripping-toast, down to where there was still access to the River; erratic turns and pauses to watch, listen. But only faint river noises or a single distant vehicle in flight roused the fog-world.

'Is there someone?'

'I don't know.'

'Following you?'

'Following us.'

'But you don't know?'

'That's right.'

They went through broken fencing and across an acreage of mouldering wharf: stores, old steam-cranes, rail tracks, perished: a sturdy weed-landscape thriving in winter. A couple of dozers, a hydraulic digger, had begun to nibble at a corner of demolition. Hennessy trod on a toppled sign, rotted, gold-leaf still clinging to it. On the jetty there was a checker's hut. They stood in its almost naked shell.

'Drink?'

'No.'

Hennessy took a mouthful of whiskey and waited for the warmth to spread. Blended in the ribs of the hut, and in the lessening fog, they could look across the sweep of wharfage, keep watch on its horizons, like commanders on high ground.

He said, 'They made railway sleepers here once. Poles for telephones too. A long time ago. Soaked them in creosote. You can smell it.'

'What are you in besides driving?' she said.

'Nothing much.'

'A thief?'

'A robber.'

'The difference is important, is it?'

'Yes.'

'Archway . . . top of the house, on the left . . .' She had a hand in the shoulder-bag again. 'Who did you ring?'

Hennessy said, 'I have a bigger gun than you think. One that fires bullets too. I could shoot your nobs off if I wanted to. I rang the robbers. Mine's in Highgate. Yours takes the pictures.'

She scanned the dim perimeter of the wharf, thought about it. 'The lawman? In business too?'

'That's right.'

'You rang Highgate. No one home?' She nodded back at Woolwich roofs barely visible. 'He might be out there.'

'Or want us to think he is.'

Across the great sweep of River the lights at Barking Creek were thumb smudges, fog ran sometimes to eddies and little ghostly whirls, floated high, showing still pools of water.

'You wanted to talk. What is it?' She viewed him with a kind of smiling impatience.

'Sadie?'

'All right. She's paid, looked-after.'

'A bolt-hole?'

'Yes.'

'A whore-master.'

'What's wrong with whore-masters?'

'You watch them. They go to the highest bidder.'

'You're well-read.'

'I know a lot of whores,' Hennessy said. 'No fuss. I pay at the check-out.'

'You're a boring shit.'

Hennessy took her by the lapels and lifted her face-level. 'You have it dead right. Boring as a dollybird's dildo, thick as a plank. That's how I like it. Now you'll run an errand for me. You owe me, darling.' He put her down, peeled off five twenties. 'That's for Sadie, from Pat. I'm paying my way, maybe yours too. Don't stay too long.'

They walked back across the blasted open space, back the zig-zag varnished streets until, in the distance, in paling grey-ness, Sadie's magic theatre took shape. He let her move on alone, stood in a doorway, drank a little, let slow dragging minutes pass him by. Then he moved for the alleyway.

The truck had been searched: truck cabs were dirty in the muck-game, untidy, but even untidiness had a pattern and it had been disturbed. Nally would have had a key, might be on the road to Highgate now. Or, maybe, only a street away, still tirelessly watching. But the cab was searched; a step nearer the target.

Hennessy reversed into the empty road, pushed for London Bridge in light barely good enough for a heavy foot on the throttle. He went by Bishopsgate, Hoxton, the Ball's Pond Road, Seven Sisters, down the back-doubles at Archway and lay on the floor of the truck until Nally had passed.

Then at a phone box he rang Rudi's number in Paddington, the threes, the sixes, the nines, and waited. It rang for a long time but Rudi answered and remembered.

Hennessy gave him the Woolwich address. 'Sadie's the guv'nor. Ask her for Kiki.'

'You been spreading it around,' Rudi said.

'Kiki. She needs a change, tell her, change of clobber. Bring her to Archway, love from Pat.'

Rudi was laughing in a high dreamy falsetto.

'Change of clobber, that's the big bit. Finger out, Rudi, foot on the boards.'

Hennessy thought of the stony eyes. He couldn't leave her a sitting duck for Nally and sheepskin. He walked past the bus stop where Cleary had stood hours before and the mini-driver had rollicked him and Kirwan was tracking. He crossed the road and climbed the steps of home. It was after five thirty.

It was fifteen minutes later, shoving for six, when Nally, back from Woolwich, stood on the forecourt at Highgate: he had driven through the Archway to note Hennessy's parked truck, the wet tyres, the dripping wings: one must always know where the pieces lie. There was a heavy four-lever mortice and a Yale on the hotel door and Nally took his keys from a small rigid leather case. The peace of the foyer, the strange living warmth of the house, embraced him. He smiled in the darkness to reassure it against danger, held out his hands and felt them touched by the aery searching fingers of Helena. She embraced him.

'You should have telephoned.'

'Yes.' He poured a little balm in the wound. 'Busy day, busy night, busy morning. Fog. Unpleasant, all of it, I can tell you. Hardly a minute.'

They went upstairs to his room; the fire shone, filled it with warmth; the pool of a bedside lamp reached his pillow, the rolled-back sheets; the room's fringes and corners were soft screens of shadow.

'You were in danger,' she said.

'Nonsense.'

'Sometimes I know.'

'But not now?'

'No, not now.' She took his coats, brought a dressing-gown and slippers. 'You haven't eaten of course. I'll make fresh orange juice.'

'Just a little breakfast,' he said.

She wore a pale blue robe and her straw-yellow hair was tied back; the beautiful sinless face was impossible.

When she had gone he thought about her for a few moments, looked at the softness of pillow and sheets, the ease of the room. He sat at his desk, wound back the ansafone tape and let it play: a few business calls, hardly urgent at that moment; and then finally Hennessy's voice. 'Archway. Top of the house, on the left. Yours under the pile. That's quits.'

He rang Mcleod. 'You weren't asleep?'

'No'

'I'm just back.'

'Long shift.'

'Yes. Around the town but everything in place. The truck driver is clever. Hennessy, you know. Just clever, that's all, nothing more. Found Cricklewood, Feehan's lodger, took her to Woolwich.'

'Woolwich?'

'A doss. Knocking-shop too and the rest.' Nally gave him the address.

'We want the girl.' McLeod seemed to mention it without importance, in passing.

'She's blondie now, a blondie whore,' Nally said. 'Flat streaky hair, black beret, red coat, tie belt. But the long legs are her own.'

McLeod would ring the nick at Woolwich on his black telephone. Nally waited while he went and returned.

'All right?'

'Yes.'

'Important? Not just a runner?'

'Important,' McLeod said.

'Good.'

He could feel McLeod's satisfaction. 'Don't worry about other business, loose ends,' he told him. 'I'll tidy things up this evening. Paddington is finished, of course. Hennessy, I imagine, dismantled the studio. He made a visit.'

'I could wind it up tomorrow then?' McLeod said. 'Hennessy, Feehan.'

'Sooner, I think.'

'Good.'

'You'll have the girl.'

'And Cleary,' McLeod said. 'Straying a bit, I told you.'

'Of course, Cleary.' Nally laughed. 'I'm always relieved when the house is tidied, and then impatient to upset it again. I'll be in touch.'

Nally changed into pyjamas, a short quilted dressing-robe, slippers. He needed a drink but not on an empty gut.

Helena brought his tray and kissed him on the cheek; he looked at her legs and thighs prancing out from the blue dressing-gown; her ingenuous face was all love. 'Orange juice, tea, crispy wholemeal toast and butter.'

'I'll be getting up about two,' he said.

'Then you'll have lunch at half past.' She composed the lunch aloud for him but he wasn't listening. He heard something about . . . nutty peppered salads that holy monks can't have . . . and laughed and said, 'Do you feel I'm in danger now?'

'I'll be back in half an hour,' she said. 'Give you time to say your prayers.' She set her face alight with a sudden enchanted wink.

Nally looked at the closed door, thought happily about her, dialled Feehan's number. It rang for a long time before Feehan answered.

'Sorry to be so early,' Nally said; he could hear Feehan's breathing. 'Are you all right?'

'Yes.'

'Heavy night last night?' For an instant Nally held out a straw of equality to him.

'Yes,' Feehan said.

'Happens to us all. I'm coming over to see you tonight. To Paddington. You'll be there?'

'Oh yes.'

'Could be a bit late. You'll hold for me, won't you?'

'I'll be here.'

'I could have a good look round. Repairs, painting, décor, all that. We could chat over a few site problems too. Days aren't long enough, are they?'

'No.'

'Hennessy, the driver fellow, he took your furniture?'

Feehan fumbled a little. 'He didn't arrive. I waited.'

'Ah! Of course you said he was a clever bastard, didn't you?'

'Yes.'

'We'll discuss him tonight.' Nally rang off, drank the orange juice, poured tea. Placing the pieces, always important, he thought again. Feehan would be 'sitting' for McLeod's pick-up; the girl would be at the Woolwich nick by now; Cleary, in McLeod's backyard, wasn't a problem. Hennessy . . .

The phone rang; he pondered a while, decided to answer. 'Yes?'

It was McLeod. 'We missed her.'

'The girl?'

'A spade driver.'

'A spade driver, blonde tart, on six o'clock roads shouldn't be hard.'

'They wouldn't miss that trick either.'

'Yes,' Nally agreed. They were silent for a little while. 'I've set Feehan up for you. Paddington tonight.'

'Good.'

'You'll arrange Cleary?'

'Yes.'

'I'll start work on Hennessy soon.' Nally thought for a moment. 'The girl might surface somewhere.'

'Possible.'

'I'm going to reassure Hennessy. He should be ready now, I think. Leave it with me.'

'Yes.'

... Nally re-ran the ansafone tape and erased it. Yes, Hennessy was a little clever. He took time to finish the modest breakfast and drank a small measure of brandy. It was after half past six: he could hear the sound of cleaners downstairs. He rang for Helena and, in the moments before she came, wrote on a sheet of notepaper, 'QUITS', addressed the envelope to Hennessy.

'Can you get a cab, a mini? Now? A discreet one, you know?'

She was looking anxiously at his slippers, pyjamas, the dressing-robe.

'I want a letter delivered.'

'Ah!' she said.

'Tell the driver there's a basement, a wino caretaker. She'll take it in.'

She smiled back at him.

'Don't be long,' he said.

Suddenly he thought of Bredin for a few moments, spiky, sour, but somehow standing in simplicity outside it all, down in the grime of Haringey soon, the phone bells jangling about him . . .

He was in bed when Helena came. She made a little sigh of regret. 'Time,' she said, 'is the enemy.' She took off the blue robe and stood naked looking at her watch. 'We can have half an hour of love and fun, that's all. Then it's sleep for you and work for me.' She got in beside him. 'I've never seen the streets at five or six o'clock, you know. Lonely, are they?'

Hennessy stood in the dark hallway . . .

The road from Woolwich in slip and patchy fog had dragged

at his energy but he had pushed on knowing that somewhere behind in the greyness Nally was dogging him; and at Archway, when he had parked, and had lain low in the cab for minutes and watched until Nally had passed on his way to Highgate, there had been a sense of grip again, a levelling of scores.

There was solace now in the darkness of the hallway and he drank a little whiskey. Rudi might get to the girl at Woolwich. He might not.

He wondered why he bothered. He thought of Sadie and her Somali stud, the outer space of River, the sad artistes of drag sleeping now beside wigs and paint and dildos. Another world.

There was no sound from Maisie's room beside him. Was Kirwan in there? Or in the nick or flat out up there on his bed? His back ached, Feehan's stony mark on his forehead was a warm distracting pulse, his stomach was tight, almost like illness.

He looked up the stair-well first, then began the slow climb.

Kirwan's room was empty, the pile untouched; but he groped down in the dirt until he felt the solid bulk of the parcel, and then carefully arranged the disorder again. He sat on Kirwan's bed. Feehan, the Paddington camera, the sheepskin man, Nally, Cleary, the girl . . . He drowsed a little, rested back against the headboard, slipped in and out of wakefulness . . .

Noise spearing up from the hallway awakened him. It was daylight, almost half past ten! He could hear Kirwan's voice, a pleading whine, and Maisie shrill as a vixen. There was a whirring sound, a slamming door, Kirwan's agonised 'Jaysus!' filling the air. Silence. He waited for Kirwan to arrive: he came, stooped, both hands on his head like a prisoner.

'For Christ's sake!' Hennessy said.

'I called in with my apologies,' Kirwan said. 'For last night. That's all!' He stood in sightless shock, holding down his scalp. 'She has a Japanese umbrella,' he said. 'She bust it on my head! Jesus, the crack, the noise!'

Hennessy saw that the Cricklewood battle had left not a mark on him. He said, 'That was your scrapyard brain rattling!'

Kirwan focused him, searched for compassion, understanding. 'I'd do anything for Maisie.'

87

'You did it all last night.'

'What will I do now?'

'Sit down,' Hennessy said; he handed him a whiskey bottle, watched him gulp at it. 'You know what time it is?'

'I was in the nick, in the dock at Willesden, only out of it! Straight here! Drunk, disorderly, a fiver. Next. All that bollicks.' He looked at Hennessy's forehead. 'I'm sorry.' He held out his hands. 'What will I do about Maisie?'

'What about Feehan?'

'I don't know.'

Hennessy took the whiskey bottle from him. 'We'll talk about Maisie when we get to her.' He waited for calmness that didn't come, only silence. 'Last night you followed Bredin's clerk. Cleary? Remember?' he stirred him. He could see in Kirwan's eyes confusion lifting like wisps on the River. 'You parked the truck and followed him?'

Suddenly Kirwan was angry. 'You bastard, Hennessy! You sent me out on that bloody hide and seek! That was it! That was the straw, that was the blast-off! Chasing a little shambling arsehole. All the way to Highbury. Walked every step of it! I drained half a bottle in cold and fog . . . half a bottle, Hennessy!'

'You said "Highbury?"'

'Highbury New Park, house like a castle.'

'His own key?'

'He's hardly in and a taxi comes. Bony looking wanker. Thin with a sheepskin.' Kirwan's impatience was in flood again.

'Tall, mousy hair?' Hennessy asked.

'That's about it!' Kirwan said. 'Now, what about Maisie?'

'Soon.'

Kirwan took a quarter of whiskey from his own pocket and had a slug. 'God bless the Pakis who never close,' he said.

Highbury, Hennessy was thinking: Cleary was the Law's nark and the Law was in Nally's pocket; bringing furniture down Feehan's steps was only to set the cameras clicking. You were on record, ready for clearance . . .

'Maisie!' Kirwan said in a huge growl.

'Sweep your own floor!' Hennessy said. 'You're knocking it off for two years. Did you put the parcel in her room?'

'Keep it respectful about Maisie,' Kirwan said.

Hennessy nodded.

'The parcel is in her room.'

'Where?'

'Everything in Maisie's room is locked. Wardrobe, drawers, suitcases, everything. I told her once if she had a pisspot there'd be a lock on it.'

'The parcel?' Hennessy said.

'Under her bed.'

Hennessy thought about it: in a world of locks and keys it might be safer there.

Kirwan drank again.

'Go easy on it,' Hennessy said. 'We're working today.'

Kirwan stared out at the daylight. 'Eleven o'clock?'

'Eleven, twelve, one, we make a show. Me for Nally, you for Feehan. No run.'

Kirwan stood reproved like a schoolboy. 'Yes,' he said. 'You're on.' He moved closer to Hennessy. 'This morning,' he began it like the lugubrious solemn opening of a prayer. 'Down there in the hall. I was going to ask Maisie for her hand.'

The dignity of it caught Hennessy unawares; he had to battle with a mad outrageous laughter bottled inside him.

'Don't, don't!' Kirwan pleaded.

'You'd have a better chance of a tenner.'

'Don't joke.'

Hennessy saw the awful helplessness; he sobered and was repentant. 'You should wait, maybe. You're stiff as a board. Let it ride till Sunday, take her to Regent's Park or down to Kew Gardens. Tell her how you feel.'

'Kew Gardens.' Kirwan's eyes flickered his anger for Hennessy. 'Kew Gardens! Christ, I'd be fine looking across a bush at Maisie, asking her to marry me, Don't, don't!' he said to Hennessy. 'I didn't mean to be funny about it. Before God, I didn't! What will I say?'

'We'll think of something.'

Kirwan gripped his arm. 'Don't walk away from me.' It was a threat and a plea; arrogance, fear, despondency, whipped into a final outburst.

'What's wrong?' Hennessy asked.

Beyond the cataclysm of Kirwan's romantic journey there might be something buried and painful that he awaited. Kirwan was afraid: he tried hopelessly to explain it, bumped like a broken wheel to a standstill. To dig a trench with his bare hands was feasible but to find words for the flimsy paralysing sweat on his mind was impossible.

'Do you ever feel bitched?' he asked.

'I don't think so,' Hennessy said.

Kirwan groaned his anguish; he flexed big flat hands before him as if the strength of them would bring reassurance. 'It's like being afraid. But of what, I don't know.'

Fear was the shiny tightness on Kirwan's face, a stranger there; it might be fear that hurried him to Maisie for some powerful towering reflection of himself.

'The job is on top of me. The first day I stepped on that site I felt old. I saw Feehan and the dirty washed-out square with grass and nettles and if there had been a five in my pocket I'd have moved us on!' He jabbed out at Hennessy. 'And when I walk the ploughed-up track to that manhole I know I'm finished. Dead. I see Feehan looking across at me with his face like a skull. I tell you there's evenings when I climb out of that hole and I'm an old man. And I have nowhere to go.'

Hennessy felt the cold gathering about them. 'You want to get your speech ready,' he said to drag him out of his pain. 'When you're hitched you'll always have a clean shirt, a suit, an overcoat in the wardrobe. Two pay packets in the week and none of them your own.'

From the hallway the quavering nasal tones of the caretaker were drifting up to them.

'Mr Hennessy . . . Mr Hennessy . . .'

There was no urgency, only a querulous moaning annoyance that she had been dragged from sleep to reality.

'Mr Hennessy . . .'

'Christ!' Kirwan tried to hurry him away. 'The noise. Maisie'll block her with the busted umbrella!'

Hennessy found her akimbo in the hallway, head raised to yelp again.

'Yes?'

She poked an envelope in his hand, said without apology. 'It come hours ago. You were gone, I thought.'

A tattered voluminous nightdress pulled about her, she shuffled off to her basement. Silence, a traffic lull, a momentary noise, an old house-groan perhaps, or Maisie creeping about in her room.

There was a single sheet of notepaper in the envelope. Hennessy opened it and read, 'QUITS'. He sat on the lowest tread of the stairs, lay against the wooden edges, let relief at last loosen, untie him. A battle past: no winners, no losers. Quits! Some nod of deference, he felt, was due to whatever haphazard providence fixed the odds. Nally would come when the house was quiet, he knew, and take his 'piece' from Kirwan's room. And Maisie's bed straddled the future. He looked at his battered hands, nodded solace to them ...

Kirwan's whisper, like the cutting slide of gravel, fell on him from the top landing. He put the letter away, climbed back to him.

'What is it?' Kirwan said.

'Not a thing.'

'You're up to your balls in trouble, aren't you?'

Hennessy drank a little, handed him the bottle. 'Just a swallow,' he told him. 'We have a day's work to do, remember?'

'We have to see Maisie!'

'Now?' Hennessy said. 'You want it now?'

Kirwan faltered to draw in wind and courage.

'Yes,' he said.

On the stairs Hennessy turned back to say, 'Cards, money and up sticks today? How would that be?'

As Hennessy rapped on the door, Kirwan said, 'Maybe I should stay out a while. Let you prepare the ground, you know?'

Hennessy grabbed him. 'It's your ground. You made it.'

Bolts were drawn, a key turned, Maisie stood pointing a shoulder at them.

'Yes?'

'Good morning, Maisie,' Hennessy said very correctly and pleased her a little.

'Morning?' she said. 'That was some time ago.' She looked out at the first tiny feathers and motes of snow dropping down . . .

'Could we have a word with you?'

And then gazed beyond him, almost in vapours of genteel loathing, at the presence of Kirwan. 'You can have a word,' she told Hennessy. She saw his forehead. 'Look at the state of you! Fighting battles for bowsies!' She left the door open and pranced back to the mirror at her crowded overmantel.

Just a shaky start: Hennessy nodded to the awful rictus of Kirwan beside him.

They moved in a step or two. 'It was my fault,' Hennessy said. 'All down to me, Maisie.'

The room had Maisie's own tenuous claim to primness and virtue; a colourless varnish with the comfort of an old wicked shade beneath it. Maisie's face was held in a cast of dainty expectation, a puzzle-face until she pushed out her lips to the stick of rouge and suddenly the tight jaws were released from their prison and it was a sensuous ageing piece of flesh, and comforting. She drew big lips for herself and put blue shade in deep sockets, made a broad V of her eyebrows; the curls of her blonde hair were tight and dry as artificial flowers.

'All down to me,' Hennessy repeated, but she was compressing her lips, sliding them back and forth to even out the rouge; she snarled at the mirror to inspect her teeth. 'God! I'm frantic with worry,' she said. 'A day's work blown to the winds and can I ever face Cricklewood again!'

Hennessy looked at the calm perfect progress towards whatever acme of adornment lived in her mind; she creamed her hands, tightened her stockings, perfumed her hair. 'Will I ever play another note!'

'He was doing a little job for me.'

'But you weren't footless with drink, were you? Or making animal noises, leaving a decent public house in a shambles?'

There was silence; Maisie put the fastidious last touches to her décor. Hennessy looked at the bed, modern but brass-knobbed for age: she had hung beribboned flimsy curtains at the head and foot, arranged flounced pillows, overlaid a dazzling floral duvet so that Kirwan must have looked betimes, on his pyre, like a battered Hindu awaiting the burning.

Hennessy had an urge to smile again but he saw that Maisie was looking at the reflection of Kirwan's doomed face in the mirror. She seemed at moments to be torn between love and loathing for him, struggling along a cold middle road of glittering hardness.

Hennessy went to stand at the window, stared out at the winter street, left them with the silence and the thawing time they needed.

Maisie was saying, 'Are you all right?'

'I ballsed up last night, Maisie, I'm sorry.'

'You don't look well.'

'No.'

'Jesus,' she said, looking at the pallor, the frightened eyes, shocked and aware of her helplessness. 'What is it?' Kirwan might be near to cracking and if grown-ups cried it was agony, real agony. When you felt that bad there should be some comfort you could turn to. She lit her gasfire, brought him close to it.

Hennessy stirred; they were unaware of him. On the street, light shone out from the shop windows, fighting the unexpected morning gloom. He watched a girl in a denim suit, woollen scarf and gloves, a shoulder-bag, short dark hair, battling with the snow-dust: long strides on long graceful limbs. As she crossed the road to the steps, he recognised her.

Maisie glanced at him as he went out to the hallway. 'A minute only,' he told her.

There was no ring on the bell or metallic rap of the letter box but when he opened the door she was standing there.

'I saw you at the window,' she said.

He looked along the kerbs. 'Rudi arrived?'

'Yes.'

Hennessy closed out the daylight; the murk of the hallway was more comforting. 'Where is he?'

'We made an odd couple, I thought. He dropped me off. The Tube. It's warmer down there.'

'A long time.'

'Warm and busy. Places to go, people to watch. Seven, eight, nine, ten, crowds everywhere.'

'Yes.'

She nodded towards the street. 'There isn't anyone out there.' The eyes never softened: they never should, he thought, or she was flagging, lost.

Maisie's head appeared at the doorway: the day was full of tenderness, surprise and delight.

'Hoo, hoo!' she gave a little twitter. 'Aren't you the cute one!' She ogled at Hennessy. 'A cuddly doll all your own, eh?'

The girl kissed Hennessy with a loud smacking sound on the cheek. 'Isn't he special?' she said.

'Come in, come in!' Maisie was agog with this impossible morning. She upraided Kirwan. 'He didn't say! Up there, cheek by jowl, and he never said!'

The girl smiled.

She remembered Kirwan and the garbled drunken exposure of Feehan at Cricklewood. But to Kirwan she was another face. And Hennessy, with a whore or a duchess! Nothing in his mounting years surprised him. He was still drawn and tight but humour was returning. At this moment all was right with the world.

'What do we call you?'

She looked to Hennessy.

'Kiki,' he told them.

'Christ!' Kirwan said. 'A stammer. You're excited.'

'Short for Katherine,' the girl said.

'Kiki. A pet name.' Kirwan nodded.

'And she is a pet!' Maisie announced. 'I wish I had a name like Kiki.'

'I'll think of one,' Kirwan said.

It was all brightness now: Maisie wagged a reproving finger for Kirwan. 'Aren't I the most awful hostess,' she declaimed. 'Not a thing in the house! Just ready for shopping, you see. But I invite everyone to breakfast. Yes, everyone.'

Even Kirwan's enthusiasm faltered in puzzlement.

'At Apollo's,' she explained to Kiki. 'A little Greek place down the way. Very select.'

She bundled them out, gentle as a shepherd; the girl took Hennessy's arm, leant her head against his shoulder. Kirwan wondered at Maisie: such resource, mastery. They huddled together in the dry whirls of snow, trotted the yards down to the amber warmth of the café.

Proprietor Stephanos, a veteran, eyed them with token welcome, a deal of circumspection: Hennessy's battle scar, Kirwan a storm signal at all times. It was the lull before lunchtime: a few ageing Mediterranean men drank coffee, smoked; a goddess girl and two Adonic boys, who might be staff, chattered and laughed from moment to moment. Maisie called for steak and French fries for the men, coffee only for Kiki, and for herself an omelette, savoury of course, with spinach and dry toast. Watching her, at first Kirwan was stunned in admiration, in awe, at her fluttering charm, her aplomb in the threat of Stephanos's professionalism. 'Large glasses of dry red each for the men.' And then a dark gloom settled on him, distanced her from him: she was beyond his bloodshot ken. The miracle of his entrée to her room, her bed, was blinding; that he had been tempted to ask for her gifted hand, monstrous, flying in the face of God. And suddenly he was reminded of her whirring rod of punishment.

Hennessy ate, raised a glass, nodded to Maisie; the girl smiled. They seemed to await some great and painful gestation from Kirwan.

'Drink your wine, dear,' Maisie told him.

'What am I doing here?' he asked her.

'Drink your wine, it's good for you.'

'Plonked before a glass of red-raddled dip! What am I doing?'

A young Adonis, a waiter perhaps, switched on music and strobe lighting; and behind Kirwan, grotesque colours sprang and danced so that he sat like a Colossus on his stage, irrevocably doomed, burning with strength and powerlessness.

Hennessy could almost feel his pain. 'The snow is heavier,' he said, looking out beyond the heat and greenery and glass.

Maisie was searching every line of Kirwan's face, finding him aged; and was sad and then happy. They might have been alone in her fussy tarted-up room.

'You haven't been looking well,' she told him.

'Are you talking about me?' He jabbed at her as if it had been an accusation, a doubt cast on his prodigious virility.

'You don't take care of yourself.'

He was looking at the neat smooth little waiter, cute as a catamite. 'I'll get a wave put in my hair tomorrow. And a pair of pants to hold my balls up.'

'You neglect yourself.'

Maisie's calm defused him. 'Oh Christ!' he said; he took the quarter of whiskey from his pocket and drank from it, feeling the burning comfort and the arrival of peace. He put the bottle in the centre of the table. Maisie's infinitely sad eyes were sad for him, he thought; and he was overcome with emotion. 'I've changed,' he confessed it to her. 'I used to fall on the pillow once and sleep like the dead. Now I awake at night with my hands out in front of me like I was afraid of the dark.'

'Afraid.' If Hennessy and the girl hadn't been there she would have comforted him and perhaps wept a little; she knew the loneliness of a room, the night-sounds of a house coming down to the darkness beside her bed. She looked at the immense strength of his shoulders and arms.

'In a few days I seem to be old,' Kirwan said.

'It's the work,' Maisie told him. 'It's too much.'

'The place,' Kirwan said quietly. 'That site is a morgue. I never saw a fight on it or a man throwing back his head to let a whoop or a shout. Feehan is like a ghost wandering about. I look up sometimes out of the manhole and there he is staring down. He might have been there half an hour. Or when I fill a skip of muck and climb up the ladder to the crane I find him standing beside it. Oh Christ, I despise him! I should maim the bastard . . .'

Maisie's eyes were full of tears. 'Chuck the job,' she whispered to him. 'Leave it behind you.'

'We're not running, are we?' he said to Hennessy.

Hennessy raised a glass to Maisie. 'Today. Our last trip,' he said.

But Kirwan, confused, unlistening, was bound fast to his fear and pain. 'When I tangle with Feehan,' he said, 'I'll finish him.' There was no assuredness about him; it was like groping for someone in darkness.

'Our last trip,' Hennessy said, his face close to him. 'Remember?'

Maisie grasped at reality, cooed her alarm. 'To work! At this hour?' she said.

'We pull our cards and money.' Hennessy tapped it out for him. And for Maisie. 'Cards and money and start again.'

Kirwan's food was untouched. The girl said suddenly to Maisie, nibbling at the edges of her omelette, 'Their last day, aren't you glad about that?'

Maisie smiled and was angry with herself. 'Here we are nattering away, forgetting we have company!' She put her hand on Kirwan's and he felt its warmth, saw her confidence and strange gentility in little nods and mannerisms.

'You look better already,' the girl told him.

The room was in sharp focus again, the whiskey bottle gleamed, the window framed for a moment the end of a lighted bus, feathers of snow, umbrellas, people in flight. Maisie was chattering, Kirwan cast in admiration. Hennessy was watching Stephanos, erect, expressionless at the stile of the counter: a big man, fleshy but powerful, a stiff shirt, oiled hair, the white smile of his teeth was an accidental splash in the colour of everything.

'Get rid of the whiskey bottle,' Hennessy told Kirwan.

But Kirwan only followed his glance to the counter, sent out the unmistakable challenge, a message of his dislike and impatience.

Stephanos came to visit them; to Maisie he said with great deference, 'Is everything satisfactory, madam?'

'Superb!' Maisie said.

Kirwan raised the whiskey bottle and took a long drink.

Stephanos said, 'You cannot do that, sir.'

'No?' Kirwan said. 'Bring us a few glasses, Jimmy, we'll all do it.'

'My name, you see, is not Jimmy.'

'I know that, Jimmy. But bring us the glasses.'

Two shirt-sleeved men, from a kitchen or a store-room,

hairy as apes, stood guard behind the counter. The last moments of the fuse to conflict were burning away. Maisie's hands trembled. Hennessy looked at the girl: she was still as wax.

'I think I can explain,' Hennessy said.

He stood up to smile his apologies, sent out reassurance to halt the battle-signal of Stephanos to his minders.

'Yes?'

'It's a special occasion.'

'Ah?'

'A proposal,' Hennessy said. 'Marriage. He was about to propose marriage. A bit difficult you see?'

Stephanos suddenly smiled, nodded at the whiskey bottle.

'Yes,' Hennessy said.

He turned to Kirwan. 'Will you stand?' he asked him and waited; and then to Maisie. 'He called this morning to ask for your hand in marriage.'

In beat noise and strobe it was an archaic ridiculous joke-bomb; but from her weathered face Maisie's eyes shone like a suprised schoolgirl's and Kirwan gazed down on her in shock, nodding his assent. The simplicity of it was blinding as a fireball. Maisie kissed him; they were standing side by side.

'Brandy,' Hennessy said to Stephanos and reached in his pocket for money.

'Don't you dare,' Maisie said. 'You and Kiki are our guests.'

Kirwan almost saluted her authority.

They drank; the girl raised her glass but left the brandy untouched. She kissed Maisie and Kirwan, came back to nestle against Hennessy. The bill was settled, money and decorous compliments exchanged. They went back through the snow.

'Perishing,' Kirwan said in the hallway and smiled in praise of his day. 'Come in and have a drink with us.'

Maisie had opened her door.

'We change. We go to work,' Hennessy said.

Maisie made a little pucker of dismay but smiled and nodded to Hennessy: he had been the saviour, the good friend. She came across and hugged him.

Kirwan had gone in. They could hear the slurp of liquor into a glass. Maisie tiptoed in pursuit. 'I'll deliver him,' she said archly, 'in two minutes. Well, maybe, three.'

From the basement came the drag of slippers, a loud yawn, the tang of tobacco.

'There's a caretaker,' Hennessy said. 'A pay-phone.' He looked at the girl, still on the run, on the trot for ever. For nothing.

Kirwan's thunderous whispering to Maisie came out to them. 'You nearly cracked my skull, God damn it.'

'I'll kiss it better.'

Hennessy called out, 'Speed it up, in there!' and pulled the door shut. 'Do you need money?' he asked the girl.

'I have all I want.'

'Good.'

'You're not running this morning?'

'Work,' Hennessy said. 'I change, I work, I pull my cards. No running.'

'You made a deal?' She waited 'Did you?'

'Yes'

'Highgate? Paid him off?'

'I have enough.'

'He might be greedy.'

If there had been an inching tide of confidence, the sharp probing assessment drained it away; she watched his hands, too restless; little moments of anger in his eyes, fighting off doubt. Highgate would swallow the offering, then him and the rest. She had no moments of compassion for him; a little pity, almost contempt.

'You're the one that's running,' he said.

'I do it every day.'

'For nothing.'

'Nothing you could bargain with.'

She was carefully back-tracking the night, examining the pieces, filling in what hours were left.

'Highgate was the watcher at Woolwich last night?'

'Yes,' he said.

'All night? A patient man.'

'Very.'

Maisie's genteel tittering and Kirwan's humour lasted a few moments and there was silence again. She watched Hennessy move impatiently, sit on the bare staircase. Above him, top of the house, on the left, was the pay-off. Collected? Hardly, she thought. Hardly. Only a guess, but a fair guess.

Suddenly she went to Hennessy, took his battered hand in her's, kissed him on the mouth, could see a moment of awful tenderness in his eyes.

'Do you think I should sit tight a little while?'

'He was standing, confused with emotion. 'With Maisie?'

'She wouldn't have to know.'

'Yes,' he said. 'Stay with Maisie till I ring.'

'Yes.'

'Till I ring. I'll fix something.'

He hammered on Maisie's door, pulled Kirwan out. 'For Christ's sake, get changed.' He pushed him at the stairs. Maisie was out, blowing kisses. The girl slipped past.

He said in hushed confidence to Maisie, 'She's in bother.'

'Kiki?'

'Keep your door bolted. I'll ring when it's clear.'

'What is it? A Man?' Maisie was ready to face fearful odds for lovers and lasses.

'A darkie,' Hennessy said. 'Beats hell out of her. That's between us. You and me.'

'Jesus!' She nodded, had to fight against a sea of outrage. From the door she said, 'Take care of my fella, won't you?'

'I'll do that.'

She was gone: a key turned in the lock, two bolts shot home.

Hennessy climbed the stairs. He thought of the stale, never-dry clothes awaiting this, the last outing, muck-smeared, oil-soaked; rolled-down rubber boots: the bleak misery of a hundred sites lived down in their depths.

At Walworth the nightwatchman drowsed a little under a makeshift canvas shelter but the cold, like a bony finger, prodded him back to consciousness; a creeping chill across his stomach and back and shoulders and then the jerk to awareness; when he awoke from a moment's sleep cold seemed to have stolen on him and he lowered himself deeper into his clothing and felt the warmth of his own breath: the fire-devil before him glowed white in midday gloom of snow and sky; he could smell the dryness of coke, but only his legs and thighs were a little warm. Site bothies were old horses' homes, he thought.

He had heard the chimes coming from somewhere up in the City and they carried the oldness of streets and brick and mortar with them. He felt his own feebleness. Always, in daytime sleep, he seemed to die a little and rallied again only when light glimmered and fell beyond the houses. The City was old in the darkness, its face limp while it slept and he watched.

He settled himself to drowse again, squinted out at the spread of the site, the wandering hem of danger lamps, dozens of red eyes, dimmed headlights of traffic catching mounds of frosted snow along the kerbs and footways, and beyond that only shadow. He was slipping away again, warmth and cold seeming to battle inside him; the magnificent ease of dropping into sleep and then the shivering instant of cold.

When he awoke it was the diesel-knock of Hennessy's truck hammering at him, pulling in across the rough unmade ground and its choking exhaust held close to earth.

He hurried away across the site, limping, stiff with the imprisoned cold in his body, towards the pub where there was warmth. In his pockets his hands were numb useless burdens.

From the cab Hennessy glanced past him, scanned the site, the perimeter, a jagged coastline of lamps and yellow tape. Snow came down steadily, leaving pipings and tilted bonnets on steel and stacked brick and timber. The site-office was dark; no car parked, no Feehan.

Kirwan, mouth open, had slumped against his shoulder, asleep. He had talked on the way, laughed, almost shouted his liberation from Archway to Bishopsgate and then, as if the crisis of some illness, a delirium, was past, a blessed sleep fell on him.

Hennessy pushed him erect, shook him. 'This is it,' he shouted.

Kirwan let the picture ripple a while and grow calm; he saw

the diminishing watchman in the sweep of snow and traffic. 'Gimpy bastard, off for a pint,' he said in a long tapering sigh.

Hennessy jabbed him before he could nod again. 'We go to work!'

'Christ, lunchtime!' Kirwan was suddenly squinting, awake, aware. 'Holy pub lights in the snow . . .'

'When Feehan comes,' Hennessy said it very slowly for him, 'he won't find pints in our fists. Just tools. No talk, no aggro.' He looked at Kirwan. 'Have you got it?'

Kirwan thought about it, pulled his jacket tight about him: moments ago, it seemed, there had been Maisie and somehow her warmth had come with him . . .

'The parcel!' He had suddenly remembered: Maisie, her brassy bed, the downy pillows, had jolted him. 'The parcel, Hennessy!'

'It's mine.'

'In Maisie's room!'

'Just a parcel,' Hennessy told him. 'Mine. Paid for. No tags.'

Kirwan rapped on the metal dash with what might be contrition, apology, doubt. 'I'm jumpy, that's all.'

'Forget it.'

'We're clear?'

'Yes.'

But he thought of Nally. At Paddington, at Cricklewood, at Woolwich; the vigil in freezing fog, the harshness, dry snow, cutting as sandblast. The patience. And then sudden retreat, capitulation. Quits. He might be greedy, the girl said. He remembered her mouth and his scabbed fist in her hands . . .

'Out!' he said to Kirwan.

They climbed down from the cab; the ground was rock hard except in the deep trenches where shovels carved out clay in dense nougat cubes and you could feel the drag on stomach and groin as it was hoisted to the surface: cables, pipes of gas and dung and water exposed, left for the surgeons to hack and by-pass; or headshake and back-fill. Another month and there might be silence and skin would grow again.

They stood like desolate figures, left to weaken and drift into the sleep of the blizzard . . .

Feehan saw them as his car crept in from the glacial inch of traffic flow; he jolted it in gear to a standstill, in a single moment launched himself. But he met the hard ground and weakness struck him like a seizure; he tried to shout abroad his instructions but the effort set off a blinding hammering pulse in his mind so that he could only cling to conciousness and rest against the open door. He felt warm and sweaty even in the icy grip of the day. Labourers, spread out across the site at their places, lived in a distant silent enclave, and he was a little shocked that they could so independently move without his own charging invective behind them. For an instant nausea flowed through his body, like drunkenness, and he fought back the urge to lean against the truck and retch. His hands were wet with sweat.

He focused Hennessy again somewhere on the pale edge of his world and called out at him; his voice was only a whisper; he was alone; he closed his eyes and breathed out the pain and weakness. Only whatever anger was left seemed to hold all his strength and he coaxed and fanned it like one red turf in the morning ashes. When he looked at the site again it was slowly coming to life about him, too lazily and slowly, but the nausea had passed and he began to move without the concentration of all his strength and will.

He went, hat down, the collar of his coat pulled up about his mutilated face where the swelling had spread and the paleness of his lips stood out like white fading grease-paint. The frost prodded into his wound, inflaming it, seeming to drag his face out of shape and he touched the swelling with his fingers. The heat was like a sudden pain against the chill of his hand.

He remembered he had held a scarf against his face in the blundering scramble from Cricklewood, running and crouching, to his car; and when he was in the darkness of his room he had drawn it gently away because it was sucked into the wound above his eye; he had probed with his fingers; there was wet blood and a soft jelly puffiness of swollen flesh rising along his face. He had switched on the light and gone across to the mirror.

Hennessy had cut him to pieces; he had done it with a single blow. The thought frightened him a little that he could so easily be stopped. There was no eye, only a mound of discoloured flesh and dried blood caked along his cheek; the wound was wide, held up and pouting over the huge swelling ...

He moved into the enveloping roar of steels and compressors, the smell of burnt oil; he held the nightwatchman's grimy lamps for his marker an instant. And then he saw Kirwan.

Kirwan, before he set listless sail for the manhole, stared back at the meaty rupture of flesh and clotted blood, drank his whiskey, flung the bottle behind him. He climbed the mound of earth about the shaft and put his feet on the ladder. Feehan examined him without pity, saw the laboured movements and drowsiness, watched his halting progress until he was down out of sight.

A cold dissatisfaction filled him. He stared out at the filthy unswept ground about the crane and the gaping shaft; and gathered strength. A man and his job were the same: the littered ground, the timber, the rust-red tubes of scaffolding, scattered muck and ballast, were the stupidity of Kirwan. He paused and looked again into the frozen mounds of disarray: a buckled trench-sheet, channelled steel, lay across a hump of ground, almost buried in hillocks of spoil and lumber.

A weapon, a gory see-saw. One end, at the manhole's edge, poked beneath the loaded skip of Kirwan's muck; the other, hardly visible, sat primed in the mix of white frozen slush. A deadly apparatus prepared for his arrival.

He steered himself across towards Hennessy, saw him lift a discarded pick from the snow, swing it and the frozen ground was ripped asunder like flesh. He measured the spread of Hennessy's shoulders. His patience slowly wasted.

'Hey!' he said. 'See all the shit your mate leaves? For you! Get your truck, bring a shovel, you thick bastard!' He seemed to hold out the awful naked wound, like a Spartan badge, for display.

Hennessy climbed into his cab.

'Move! Move!'

In the driving mirror, Hennessy saw the wedge face, shrunken, distorted, the smeared stylish hat askew, the blood-ied duffel; and suddenly there was compassion for Feehan like the grey sadness of winter light; something had shaped and obsessed him, turned him loose, and he fought savagely to destroy it. Hennessy pushed the starter.

Feehan's immense hands, in the mirror, beckoned him, guided him, reversed him in tight, breaking the frozen crust and ploughing into the loose muck and sand. The big double wheel found the steel sheet, for a moment sent it riding before it, and then the heavy threads of the tyre gripped it, pushed it down. Hennessy saw it rear up suddenly and the huge steel skip slithered away from it, vanished into the manhole . . .

He was rushing towards the ladder; he could hear Feehan shouting behind him. On the floor of the shaft Kirwan was face downwards, his head and shoulders buried.

Feehan's shouts, like keening, cheering, rang out across the site: a madness.

Hennessy went down and levered the skip aside and scooped away the muck until he met blood and the white shattered mess of Kirwan's head. He climbed back up to Feehan.

'Dead?' Feehan asked.

Hennessy thought he should kill him; it would be satisfying to drag Feehan down and bury his face in the slush of rotten death.

'YOU killed him,' Feehan said.

He had turned, was waving his instructions across the site. The crowd was gathering. Hennessy lay against the wing of the truck, felt himself trembling; he seemed to drowse. A police car, a whirring shrieking wail, bored its way to them through a solid balk of traffic; and an ambulance. There was a hush on the site; the machinery was silent.

They would take Kirwan up from the manhole, a body and a huge dome of cotton wool, somewhere probe at him a while, rest him in a morgue; tomorrow there would be a whip on site, a pound, two, a five, a ten, to coffin him and send him to the two-up-two-down oblivion of Leytonstone. The great plan seemed nothing beside a mutilated body, even the ageing, almost spent, body of a failure. Kirwan had been honest. For a moment he thought of Maisie . . .

A police sergeant, very quiet, tired too perhaps, was saying, 'You didn't see the obstacle, the raised end?'

'It was buried.'

'You didn't feel it?'

'I thought I might be riding a stone, a piece of concrete.'

'He drove the crane?'

'He climbed up to drive the crane.'

'He was responsible?'

'Yes.'

It went on: the carelessness of Kirwan, the confusion, the dirt, the litter, steel sheeting left mindlessly on the deck. A man dead in his own stupidity.

'He was dead when you went down?'

'Yes.'

He seemed pulled apart from it, confused by the shock that was maturing now and spreading through his body. If Feehan wanted to lay bare the underbelly, the pale underneath skin, he too had made it with a single blow. He thought how easy it should be to kill Feehan and feel no trace of guilt. Kirwan's belongings were brought; a few pence, cigarettes, matches; an accident card that had been pinned in his pocket; he was a Catholic, send for a priest, inform next of kin. Maisie had written her name, address, phone number with a spidery dash . . .

'Company vehicle?' the Law asked.

'Yes.'

'Insurance?'

'They'll send it.'

'Licence?'

'Yes.'

'There'll be a statement.'

'Yes.'

'Where's the gaffer?'

Hennessy pointed across at Feehan: the bright shoes were painted in mud now, the face a grisly mask; the hat.

'Always looks like that, does he?'

'He just arrived,' Hennessy said; he put his scarred hand out of sight.

In the snow, groups all about, hardly moving, might have been clumps of scrub on a bare wasteland. There was a telephone box on the pavement and he moved across to it, thinking with a timeless banality of the inconsequence of them all. The ambulance men passed him: the covered stretcher, Kirwan's muck-stained boots shaking from side to side. Nothing was so dead as dead feet.

He telephoned Bredin that there had been an accident; Kirwan, a heading driver, was dead; and Bredin was listening without comment. He was guarded, Hennessy thought: there might be someone at his shoulder.

'The Law want the insurance.'

'Mmm.'

'You'll send it?'

'Yes.'

Bredin, cautious and distant: there was something there to ponder and perhaps discover but it was lost in the confusion. Maisie, he remembered again like a sudden gut pain. And the girl. He pulled his donkey about him and felt the bulk of the gun at his hip! The gun ... the Law! Christ, everything shifting beneath his feet! There was an urge to run from it all, in thundering roaring shame from Maisie, the girl, the parcel. From Kirwan.

'You all right?' the Law man had loomed up before him.

'Insurance,' Hennessy said. 'I rang for the insurance.'

'Good. Where's this gaffer's drum?'

'Paddington.'

'Do him a favour. Get him there.'

Hennessy nodded.

'Then back to the nick, we'll do the statement. How's that?'

The Law pulled away. Feehan, the door open, sat in the driving seat of his car, glazed in sweat. Hennessy looked at the whole Christmas card world of the site. The groups had scattered. Kirwan's leaving had been silent as the snow. Everything must be silent as the snow, he thought. Now was the test.

He went across to Feehan's car, crashed into the driving seat, sent Feehan sprawling against the nearside door and window, let him slide down to the floor. The wound at his eye had opened again and the blood oozed down his face to his collar. He was motionless, might have slept. Hennessy wanted to drink; but there was time enough for drink; no slips for the

Law; Kirwan was dead, the rest was intact.

He pushed on to London Bridge and beyond it the roads loosened a little. He went by Moorgate into the ghost world that had once been Hoxton ...

Feehan was stirring, suddenly groping, levering himself to the seat. A growth of hand sprouting from the heavy gold band of a wristwatch mopped at blood. He put his hat carefully on his knees and raised the cowl of his duffel to hide his face: he was an image of death or inquisitor or both.

'Accidents happen,' he told Hennessy, laboriously tying words together. 'To careless bastards. Don't forget it.'

Hennessy remembered Kirwan and Stephanos, the Apollo breakfast, Maisie's glory ...

'I'm warning you,' Feehan said.

And Maisie would weep now for the outlandish dream she had woven, that time and reality could never blemish; a little whiff of gin on her breath, bright eyes, and remembering Kirwan forever.

'Accidents are always happening.'

'Jesus!' Hennessy shouted. Everything was an explosion of pity and hate. 'You're nothing, Feehan, nothing! I could kill you. Now. Not with an iron bar or a crane skip. With my hands. But I'm sorry for you.'

'Not sorry, gutless.'

Kirwan had been everyone, searching, peering under stones, for contentment.

'You're a mouth, that's all,' Feehan said.

Hennessy pulled into the deserted white acres between tower blocks, stood on the brakes. He grabbed at Feehan's throat, pinned him on the seat, watched the monster hands clawing, flailing, weakening. Feehan's eyes stared up helplessly, his mouth gaped.

'Out!' Hennessy shouted at him. Suddenly he found himself weeping for Kirwan. 'Out, out! Oh Jesus!' He opened Feehan's door, put a boot against him and kicked; he heard the thud of Feehan's landing.

Snow came down unhurriedly on what had been the streets of Hoxton, the market, the shops, the boozers, The Green, the

Friar's Church. Feehan lay still where he had fallen. Hennessy walked round, took the gun from his waist, cleaned it, put it in Feehan's pocket.

It wasn't yet half past one; lunchtime still, the caffs, the boozers, busy everywhere, here, down at Walworth, at Archway, at Highgate. Was Nally at Highgate? Or in Archway for payment? He thought of Bredin, Cleary, the girl. And Maisie. Nothing had changed, only Kirwan was dead. He took the half-flask of whiskey from his pocket and sent it looping out over the snow; he heard the muted sounds when it shattered.

He got in Feehan's car and turned again for the River and the Law at Walworth.

Maisie said, 'Do you like it?' She spread her arms to unfold the curios and geegaws of her room. The gasfire made a dull fluttering noise.

'It's lovely,' the girl said.

'I've built it up,' Maisie admitted.

'It's lovely.'

'Everything means something, you see?'

'That's how it should be.'

'Bill likes it too. That's his name.'

'I'm glad you're happy,' the girl said.

Maisie, charged with a rebirth of energy, turned on an old Bakelite valve-radio; it was battered, the knobs long gone, replaced with butts of bottle-corks. 'Bill gave me that,' she said. 'The week I met him. Over two years now. Repaired it too. He's very handy.' She saw the girl was standing carefully back from the window, watching the snow that seemed to diminish and then attack in flurries. 'Funny, isn't it,' she said, 'hearing all that black music inside an old wireless?' She switched it off.

The girl smiled.

'Should be Billy Cotton, Palm Court or something.'

'Yes.'

Maisie searched for words or employment: she moved about in a spool of sound with her hoover, told the girl as she passed,

'He said keep you safe,' had a smile in return. Well, no prying, everyone's business their own, Maisie thought. She tired of hoovering, took paper and a Christmas pen – Good wishes: the Spotted Dog: Al & Bee – and wondered about her trousseau. She was filled with words and excitement; and she was alone.

The girl listened to her movements, watched her sometimes, thought of Hennessy, the staircase to the top, the room on the left. There had been no arrivals or departures. Highgate would come for his bundle. But how soon?

Maisie's door was double-bolted, locked, the key in the lock. A few minutes out of her gaze – the hall, the stairs – and it was done.

'Bathroom?' she asked.

'First landing.'

The girl smiled.

'There's a chamber pot in the locker.' Maisie briefed her with a certain delicacy. 'Everything we want here. Fire away, love, don't mind me.' She pointed to a basin and ewer, soap, a towel. 'Keep ourselves to ourselves.'

'Later,' the girl said.

Maisie smiled understandingly at the silences. 'You got yourself a real man,' she said once. 'Hennessy's a real one. Give him time, he'll ring you. A couple of hours, maybe, but he'll ring.'

The girl let it ride. 'We'll hear it all right?'

'Easy,' Maisie said. 'Or she will.' She pointed at the basement. 'Nosey. Does the answering sometimes, comes rapping on doors.'

She polished her hands in sudden decision, put on knee-length boots, a tweed coat, woollen hat and gloves. 'I'll only be half an hour,' she said. 'Jones's at Holloway. Only down the road. A bus there and back.' And she confided. 'I'm silly, aren't I? Going-away stuff, you know. Just a look, that's all. You'll be all right. Keep your door bolted, love.'

'Wish I could go with you.'

'A pity, isn't it?' Maisie said. 'Don't be anxious, he'll ring. You got ages, love!' She looked at her watch. 'Only after half past one, you see? With the boozers open, you know, Walworth might be a long journey for that pair.' She laughed happily about it all. 'I wonder what Bill's thinking now?'

'Of you, what else!' the girl said, willing her on her way.

'Wait!' Maisie halted. Suddenly she was motionless, listening.

'What is it?'

'Don't you hear? The door, footsteps in the hall? It's Bill!'

'There's nothing . . .'

Maisie fought with lock and bolts, threw open the fortress. She ran into the empty hallway, stood gazing at the cold peeling walls, looked towards the basement, the stairway rising up. The girl stood beside her. There were faint sounds from the snow-world outside but the house was in stillness. Even the basement.

'That you, Bill?' Maisie sent her prettiest words tinkling up from landing to landing.

'There was nothing.'

She looked at the street door. 'I heard it shut! And his footsteps. I should know his footsteps, shouldn't I?' She turned and caught the girl's face in a moment of tenderness. 'I even thought he called me . . . but now I'm not sure . . .'

'You're hooked,' the girl said. 'Really hooked.'

Suddenly Maisie was laughing. 'A bit old to be giddy, love.' She nodded to her room. 'In you go. Out in the snow for me and off to Jones's! I must be mad!'

On the threshold, the girl planted a little kiss on her nose. She closed the door, pushed home the bolts, called out, 'Take your time. I'm safe as houses.'

'See you soon, love,' Maisie was saying.

The girl heard the key turned from the outside, Maisie's prim footsteps and the slam of the hall-door. There was silence.

Her anger, aimed at herself, suddenly flared and died: she should have clubbed the silly old bitch, left her asleep. But there had been an easy silent way – it was still there – and it had beckoned. She looked at the keyhole of the mortice for minutes, even drew the bolts and tested. It was tight as a drum. The window was immovable, glued hermetically by dust and damp and years; even beyond broken glass would be the long drop to the basement. Too long. She had hung her shoulder-bag on a

III

chair. The gun: one, two shots in the mortice. She listened and for the first time heard sounds of cutlery and delf from the basement. She waited: the draining away of anger, impatience, took time. The trick was, waiting. Waiting for the moment and grabbing it. It would come. In twelve hours there had been a lot of waiting.

Maisie's long nets — hangings, she called them — were suspended from brass rings on a pole. The girl took her place behind one, arms folded, patient, hardly moving. The window glass shone from Maisie's care but, outside, the brown wash of a decade clung like tissue: the steps up to the street door, down to the basement, were beside her, below her. In her sights. And Highgate too if he made his call. Beyond that there was no plan: it would be move for move. The snow fell steadily, distanced the pavements, the huckster frontages of the opposing shops.

She thought of Maisie's chichi bed and the smell of Kirwan, the brass balls, the battered frilly pillows at the heel of a hunt. The mantelpiece was a crowded trophy shelf of her junketing safaris to Southend Pier, Margate, Canvey, Brighton, Clacton, Bognor, even the distant galaxy of Penzance and Penrith. And was this the end? Kirwan's horizons would be across the road or perhaps a street away. She thought of the pot in Maisie's locker: it would have flowers and delicacy surely, not some grinning logo on its bottom . . .

She let time flow without a torrent or a ripple; an hour might have passed, unmeasured; the snow was a fine powder again; Maisie's departing footmarks on the steps had vanished. There was a phone ringing but she stuck by the window; it was answered; the bell ceased, she heard the floppy steps of the caretaker descending. And she immured herself in frozen stillness again.

At some time a rocket burst in the grey curtain above the roofs; the coloured stars had hardly shone when they were gutted. It would be a bad night for bonfires . . .

School-children were appearing now, pinched ones, paler than snow, plodding, hobbling, beside great enshrouded protectors; little knock-kneed ones hunched at the bus stop.

It took an immense practised patience to stay spirit-like in a motionless frame by the window; but it was an isolation from fear or anger. Only the vigil was important . . .

Three fleshy boys, hardly in their teens, bulls and pack-leaders of the future, were suddenly on the pavement. A snowball exploded on the glass before her; and again and again. A hail of snowballs. The window frame rattled with the force, the glass might shatter. She had instinctively recoiled from the opening thuds but recovered and stood looking at the opaque slithering mass in motion. She could hear the cheers of the ambush in flight. The battle was over. In a minute, perhaps less, the street was visible again. Uncertainty prodded at her: in the half-light of the room, a careful exact distance from Maisie's curtain, she was hidden from view. But the featureless window, nets and gloom, seemed a bright shining target for the little yelling in-and-out guerrillas; they had trampled the steps to the hall door, to the basement, scooped up snow for the blitz. It was a pause of thirty blind seconds, leaving puzzlement, disquiet.

And then another sudden twist of surprise. An explosive blow-torch burst of sound from the basement: a television, a radio, plugged in, the volume left open, tearing, distorting at maximum. Ten, fifteen seconds and it was adjusted: there was soft music, distant, muted, and the whining grumble of the caretaker.

The girl rushed to the locked door, held an ear against it, listened for a movement. A footfall, the groan of an ageing tread on the stairs? There was nothing . . .

Almost at once Maisie arrived.

She heard her in the hallway and went through the motions of drawing the bolts. Maisie turned her key and stood laden with parcels, flushed, glowing, overspilling with youth in her winter coat, her woollen hat gently dusted, decked with snow. She was a little tipsy.

She said, 'God, I'm a cow, love, a proper cow! Went on a spree!' She dumped the parcels on the bed. 'Shop, shop, shop! A pizza and then, would you believe it, a glass of wine! A table at the window too. And then I remembered the time . . .'

Maisie was unstoppable; the girl smiled. 'Everything is fine,' she told her.

'Christ!' Maisie shouted; she rushed at the door, slammed it, bolted it, locked it. 'Did he call?'

'There was a call,' the girl said.

'But she didn't come rapping?'

'The caretaker?'

'She didn't come rapping or calling, did she?'

'No.'

'Then it wasn't him.' She was suddenly relieved. 'I took a taxi back. God, how time flies. Wait till you see!'

She began to open parcels: a powder-blue coat, teetering navy shoes, a straw boater festooned in fruit and foliage; underwear, night clothes . . .

'I don't think he'll make it,' the girl said.

'Hennessy?'

'I'll leave an address. You can tell him where to find me.'

'He's pissed, love! Pissed! Him and Kirwan out of their minds! It's a big day!'

'Still, it's time to go.' She readied herself, stood with her hand deep in her shoulder-bag.

Maisie came across, palms held out to her. 'You'll look at my coat first, won't you?' It was a special plea. 'It's how I'll be on the day, you know. I'd like you to see it, to tell me . . . ' She took the key from the door, put it on the mantelpiece.

'Why not?' the girl said, calm, easily persuaded; she took each moment as it came, negotiated from minute to minute. Maisie on a hair-spring. It might be disaster to alarm Maisie. 'You're right,' she said. 'He'll ring, he's special.'

'Of course he is.'

'I'll wait.'

She sat on a fragile dainty chair while Maisie dressed: the coat and shoes had a certain Whitsun dash about them but the hat was an outrage. Maisie was suddenly music-hall, darling of the pits, over the top, a hell-raising hussy.

'What do you think?'

The girl said, 'The coat and shoes are wonderful, but the hat is a dream. Bill will love it.'

'You think so?'

'It's a winner!'

'God, I'm relieved,' Maisie said. 'He's not used to style, you know.'

And then she paused, seemed to battle with herself and finally capitulate, threw caution to the winds. From her handbag she took the little purple box and held out her engagement ring.

The girl went to her, hugged her, kissed her.

'A hundred and fifty,' Maisie said; she looked at herself and at her purchases. 'I went to the bank, that's what really kept me, love.'

'Bill's a lucky man,' the girl said.

'He'll make it up to me. Ten times over. You don't know my Bill.'

She paraded and pranced about a little, stood at her wardrobe mirror and made faces, and finally breathed out her satisfaction with the day. She sat, freeing the skirt of her coat, and stretched her legs. 'I'm whacked.'

'Yes,' the girl said after a long silence. 'Bill will love it.'

'God . . .' Maisie mumbled; she was nodding; her shoulders dipped, her hands on her lap groped a little and splayed. She drifted away.

The girl looked at her watch, waited in silence while five minutes passed, and took the key: slow grinding progress, noiseless; the bolts, the lock, the careful probing steps to the hallway, the closing of the door. The muted music barely reached her from the basement.

She looked at the stairs, motionless, hyping like an athlete for the take off. On the landing, half-way up, she rested and listened. There was no sound.

'Hennessy,' Cleary was saying to Bredin at Haringey. 'He writes a good hand.'

He had arrived early, before ten o'clock, clean, hair tidied, almost groomed except for the sprouting fingernails, shoes that had never seen polish. And he had been busy: store-cards, bins, time-sheets, files. Now, in the warmth, looking out beyond

Bredin at the swirl of snow and the awful gelid ugliness of machinery, he was in the perusal of his logsheets.

'Busted speedo.'

'We know,' Bredin said.

Bredin was faintly pleased with him, and he remembered that yesterday Cleary had seen Hennessy at Manor House and there had been importance somehow attached to it; importance for Cleary.

'A fair driver,' Bredin said. 'A head on his shoulders.'

'Not the type, is he?'

Bredin listened.

'Seems wrong, you know? Too good. Dress him up, he'd look like a guv'nor. And talking rough is hard work for him, I think sometimes, but you meet all sorts.'

'You do,' Bredin said.

'A man's business is his own.'

'It is.'

'I don't think he drinks a lot. A cagey man.'

It was the aimless exchange of come day, go day, even a waste of words but, beyond the banality, Bredin could sense, like an abrasive mica grain of sand, the impingement of purpose. The little bastard was up to something. He threw out a line for him.

'Sometimes the good ones need watching.'

'Yes,' Cleary said.

'He was a bit off course yesterday, too.'

'Well off.'

'Watch him. He might be tricky.'

'Might even have form?' Cleary let the question spiral away on the gasfire's pulses of heat, listened for Bredin's reaction.

Bredin ignored it, rolled a dark moist cigarette and waited. As you grew older, he thought, everything prepared itself for a departure; even taste rushed on ahead and left only remnants for the final days. He smoked. He hadn't seen the green fields beyond the spill of London for thirty-five years – and then from the train – and he wouldn't want to see them again. He had rid himself of want and insecurity but it was too late: dragging his fat body over places where he had run, looking for thirty-five-year-old laughter, could only be sad, he thought. He looked at

Cleary who was helpless, almost a fool, and felt a little drag on his allegiance: he had pulled loneliness about himself and abruptness and embitterment and found satisfaction that he was his own world, a maker of heavens and hells as he required them. But Cleary intruded: he pitied him, worried about him, perhaps loved him a little. He could punish him too . . .

'I'll do that,' Cleary said.

'What?'

'Watch him. He might be tricky.'

'Yes.'

Bredin looked out at the snow-covered filth of machinery, the icy metal. There were times when he sat at the window of his yard, when the day was just new and fresh, and rolled his first cigarette and wrote in his diary, 'A beautiful morning.' People saw it there, fitters, blacksmiths, drivers, welders, sweepers, and were amused. Bredin and a beautiful morning, dear Christ!

'I'd like to go about four today?' Cleary said.

Bredin looked at him. 'That's why you came in early.'

Cleary laughed. 'No,' he lied. 'I need a check-up. Nothing serious. I've let myself go. I'll pay the quack a visit.' He looked at Bredin's fat ageing face with kindness stuck on it and saw an undiscovered ugliness. Bredin had glutted all his vast appetites and this was the last one, the need to give succour and advice, to feel hardness thawing in such a brilliant sun. Cleary loathed him: it was pleasant to prod and exploit him in small remission of his harassment . . .

And there would be time, four till six, to get at Hennessy's doss, turn it over. Thinking of it, he was almost breathless in fear and excitement.

The telephone rang; Bredin lifted it. It was Hennessy: there had been an accident; Kirwan, a heading-driver, was dead. He listened without comment.

'The Law want the insurance.'

'Mmm.'

'You'll send it?'

'Yes.'

He hung up. There had been a feeling that some schemery, big or small, had been woven about him, unseen; he was of no

117

matter, it seemed, a great flabby unimportance. And he was failing, everything in his body a little weary and suffocated.

Cleary said, 'Is Hennessy long with us?'

'I forget,' Bredin told him.

'He didn't come from a poke or a water-logged cabin.'

Bredin was standing, pulling a donkey jacket across the great span of his shoulders. 'Come on,' he said to Cleary. 'I'll buy you a lunch.' He strode down through the graveyard of machinery, out to the pavement where his car stood, gift-wrapped in snow; underneath, it was dirty, the bodywork neglected, perished; but the engine was a soft throb of power. Bredin cleared the windows with his bare hands, sprayed spirit on the film of ice. 'Come on!'

'Where?' Cleary disliked the litter at his feet, the smell of oil.

'A mile or two.'

Bredin drove into the seamy skirt-tails of Tottenham: a pub sitting like a stately old manor on its grounds and parterres of tarmac. The car made virgin tracks to the rear, an exposed compound of snow and frosted chain-link. Night-time and weekends the tills would ring; lunchtime, it was a turnover of middle-aged pints, fast food, little topless girls stomping and grinding to beat music. Bredin bought whiskey and pints of beer and put Cleary sitting where he must face the bobbing dollymop heads, the little bouncing knobs of flesh.

'He isn't the type at all.'

'Who?' Cleary said.

'Hennessy.'

Cleary suddenly heard himself in what might be mimicry; he said harmlessly, 'He isn't the type you get shovelling much into lorries. Grafting for dossers like Feehan.'

'You're right,' Bredin said. 'Now drink your whiskey.'

Cleary smiled. 'I never do. Juice, that's the limit. You can sup that lot yourself, I'm afraid. Not for me.' He looked at the pints, the little tot glasses beside them, glowing amber.

Bredin tipped the whiskey into one glass. 'Drink it,' he said. 'Lift it up and drink it.' Beneath the table his hand tightened on the soft flesh at Cleary's groin: Cleary's pain was like a little tittering thread of sound. 'Drink it. Straight up, straight down!'

The glass chattered against Cleary's teeth.

'Down.'

The explosion of fire and torment left him gasping for air; he gripped the edges of the table for ballast. Bredin released him.

Slowly he was regaining pulse and vision.

'You know a lot about Hennessy,' Bredin said.

He retreated before the suddenness of it; Bredin's hand tightened on his wrist now.

'You must give him a lot of your time. Do you watch him? Drink your beer lad.'

Cleary worked at it, felt gorge swelling, rising. 'I'm going to be sick,' he said. 'Christ, get me out of here!'

Bredin saw his eyes, dull, full of yellow pain. He jerked him to his feet, propped him out past the featureless lunchtime drones, to the compound. 'Keep your mouth shut tight on it. And stand up straight.' Before they could reach the car Cleary leant against the brick wall and spewed and gawped his illness.

Bredin, in the pale silky snow, stood watching him, searching for anger, fighting the pity that rose up instantly: the spent shoulders, feet apart, hands flat and pale against the dirty brickwork. He wanted to be angry enough to beat terror into him but there was only compassion in his mind and the longing to find him innocent. He was so incompetent, inadequate.

Cleary wiped his face and made to walk towards the car.

'Wait!' Bredin said.

But Cleary kept on walking and Bredin strode after him, pushed him back against the wall: he saw him almost in tears, frightened and sick.

'Answer me, do you hear?' Bredin said. 'Are you a bloody little informer?'

'No.'

'You have all the stinking smell of one.'

'I'm not, I tell you!'

'What are you watching Hennessy for?'

'I'm sick, I tell you!'

'Aren't you watching him?'

'No!'

Bredin pinned him against he wall with his fist, looked about at the emptiness. 'I don't give a fiddler's fuck for the Law, theirs or mine, or a whole shithouse of greedy guv'nors. Do you hear? Not a dosser's clinker for anyone. But if you're an informer, I'll beat you senseless. You brainless little chancer. You prodded at me all day, thought you were clever enough to pump me. I was easy on you and you tried to get on my back. You little bastard, you're an informer, aren't you?'

'No . . . I swear it!'

'Aren't you?'

'No . . . no . . .'

'What are you?'

'I can't tell you.'

'You'll tell me all right,' Bredin said. He stood back and brought a fist on a level with his face. 'I'll straighten you out now. Or finish you.'

'I can't tell you . . . Oh Christ, Bredin, don't hit me! I'm not the one to blame.' Cleary wept and then for an instant, like a frantic miracle, through all the heaving fear and humiliation, he saw hope!

'I'll tell you.'

'Go ahead,' Bredin said.

'Hennessy is an informer.'

The brilliant unexpectedness of it silenced Bredin; he floundered but in a split second he was convinced, standing there, lowering his fist. 'Hennessy,' he said. 'Oh crucified Jesus!' He was ashamed and wanted to pull Cleary towards him and comfort him. 'You're certain?'

Cleary wept aloud and hid his face in his hands. 'I have to watch him. That's my bit.' He was trembling in the aftermath of fear; or it might be in the satisfaction of having outwitted the enemy.

Bredin gazed, in awe, at the grotesque little hero, worn, without reward, playing a deadly game. He loved him.

'I'm sick,' Cleary said. 'And cold. I want to sit a while.'

Bredin put his arm around him, led him to the car. They drove back through West Green and on to Bredin's room at Turnpike.

'Where are we going?' Cleary asked.

'You can rest a few minutes,' Bredin said.

Cleary watched the street names, located himself: there was a scrap-yard at the corner of Bredin's road, a crane and debris spilling into the street, a phone box. It was dead and featureless as a brown postcard of the past.

'I'm all right,' Cleary said. 'I won't come in.'

'You'll sit for half an hour.'

There was no escape. Bredin opened the battered door: hardboard nailed across broken panels of glass. At a pay phone in the hall he wrote down the number for Cleary and pushed it in his pocket.

Cleary moved ahead of him on the stairs, dreading even the touch of the gross fleshy hands.

'I'm all right.'

'A few minutes.'

Bredin's room was a dingy stage-set, sparse as the absurd, awful even to Cleary's apathetic survey: an iron hospital bed, a table, a chair, no more; he had nailed a curtain across his window; a single garment, a raincoat hung on the door.

'A cup of hot tea.' Bredin lit an oil stove in the corner.

'No!' Cleary almost shouted. A twin-ringed electric stand sat on the table; a kettle, a mug, a plate, a knife and fork; not even a spoon; a frying pan of pale congealed lard.

Bredin capitulated. 'Just sit and rest.' He switched on a bare ceiling light and, robbed even of the shelter of dusk, a glare of loneliness sat on everything. If, some evening, the ambulance came and took Bredin whirring down the roads to Holloway, all trace of him might be obliterated in moments . . .

He had seated Cleary and stood, motionless, at the window.

'When did you tumble him? Hennessy?'

Cleary was very careful. 'I wasn't sure until yesterday.'

'You saw him at Manor House?'

Cleary paused long enough to establish protocol, the parameters of confidence; eventually he conceded. 'Yes.' Bredin would keep his distance.

Bredin nodded. 'You'll get someone to handle it? To handle Hennessy?' He paused for a moment. 'Feehan at Walworth, he's the man.'

'The cowboy's hat?' Cleary said: it was a dismissal.

'Ring him.'

Cleary was silent.

'Christ!' Bredin said, angry for a moment. 'I'm worried for you! Who's Kirwan?'

Cleary was suddenly stirring. 'Walworth,' he said. 'A heading-driver, a tunneller.'

'He's dead.'

Behind a pale sickly mask Cleary was startled; but silence, caution, patience, were the prods to keep Bredin in check.

'A skip of muck dropped on him,' Bredin said. 'Hennessy's truck.'

Cleary thought about it: it seemed fortuitous, isolated but he said, 'Kirwan dosses at an Archway kip. Hennessy too.' It took a neat shuffle to make it as tangled as possible for Bredin. 'Kirwan's a latch, a piss-merchant. Might have got nosey, stumbled on something.'

Bredin said, 'There's a phone in the hall. Ring someone. Your bit's done.' He wondered at the sudden calm, the acuity of Cleary.

'Where's Hennessy?' Cleary asked.

'The Law at Walworth . . .'

'His room at Archway. I need to get there. Important.' He stood and tidied himself. 'I'm going now.'

'Wait,' Bredin said. He gave him twenty pounds. 'You'll ring me. If there's bother. Remember that.'

Cleary nodded.

'Say it!'

'I'll ring you.'

Bredin might have hugged him; but he guided him gently to the stairs, listened to his footsteps; and then, from the window he watched the frail heroic figure out of sight . . .

And Cleary could feel Bredin's sickly stare at his neck and shoulders. He rounded the scrap-yard, out of sight. He took the telephone number from his pocket, tore it savagely, trampled it in the snow.

Kirwan dead at Walworth. Hennessy's truck: a ton of muck and metal tumbling, dropping twenty feet on to flesh and skull

122

and clay. Kirwan was a slob, a messer, something to sacrifice maybe, he thought, but hardly a target. It was out of joint, a distraction. He pushed it aside.

He hurried and near Turnpike Station he took a taxi to Archway. The smell of Bredin's meat-fed body, his breath, warm, burdened with fat and tobacco tang, lived on with Cleary. He remembered the brick wall and the vomit about his feet, Bredin's fist, the drink, the savagery; and then the cloying descent to sweetness. He looked at Bredin's twenty pound note, spat on it, folded it away carefully. Christ, he had baffled the fat bastard: and, in desperation, the Hennessy move had been a side-step of genius. He was happy, even in the still-lingering springs of illness.

He paid the taxi at Junction Road. The snow was resting a little and an icy breeze came in sudden stabs. He went carefully down the hardening slush of the footways, vetting his entry street by street. There was no truck. Hennessy was at Walworth still or somewhere on the long creeping road.

Cleary passed the Apollo of Maisie's mad epithalamic breakfast, the bus shelter, the minicab shop, the Greek face that had abused him. Darkness was falling early; a few rockets distantly exploded.

He stood and looked across at the house: except for the basement, it was in darkness.

A bus passed, ploughing through the roadway quagmire, and he crossed in its wake. The steps to the hall door, the basement steps, were trampled and scooped of snow, as if there had been a recent plethora of comings and goings. It seemed odd and he wondered about it; across the basement area he saw the smears and remnants of the schoolboy ambush on Maisie's window. He had a moment of doubt, he smelt danger, but the die was cast. His disposal of Bredin had bred arrogance and a sudden flood of hubris to carry him along.

He tapped on the basement glass and the door opened on a chain to show half the caretaker's face. He could smell the liquor on her breath and it almost sent his stomach into spasm.

'What do you want?' she said.

'There's a driver, Hennessy, here.'

'In two, three hours maybe.'

Cleary put his foot in the door. 'I'm from the office. There's been an accident.'

'Is he dead?'

'He's all right,' Cleary said.

'How many did he kill?'

Cleary was silent; she looked at his smallness, the lack of substance, and opened the door.

'One person killed,' Cleary explained. 'A street accident. Bad weather, treacherous roads, you see? Someone like yourself popping out to the shops and suddenly it's over.'

There was a punished litre bottle of plonk on the table and dregs in a glass: the whole room seemed to be stood on its hackles behind her; she drained the wine.

'He sent me for his licence,' Cleary said. 'It's up there. His room.' He offered her a sad bona fide smile. 'He's with the Law, you understand? A bit urgent.' He went past her to the house door. 'I'll be a minute or two, that's all. I know where to find it.'

She was whining something at him and he shut her off in mid-sentence, crept, swift and cautious as a mouse, past the telephone and by the door to the hallway. He stood preparing himself for the ascent. There was only the dragging of feet from the basement, the clink of a glass; and silence.

But he hadn't heard her parting shot: that Nally had already arrived.

Nally had awakened at two, as he intended, but he heard the arrival of Helena and closed his eyes again to give her the little importance of rousing him. She kissed him and patted his face gently.

'Yes, my dear.'

'Two o'clock.'

'You're wonderful.'

'You slept well?'

'Dreamless.'

'The quiet conscience sleeps in thunder.' She kissed him

again. 'Lunch in half an hour. What will you wear?'

'I haven't thought about it. I'll manage. You're busy.'

She nodded, hurried away.

Nally enjoyed each moment of his ablutions, emerged in warm unhurried concentration. Helena had set his table and a waitress brought fresh grapefruit juice, very bitter, poached salmon, ungarnished, unsauced; and Helena's wicked salad. When he was alone, he pondered, drank the juice and left only tiny scraps of his meal.

And now Hennessy.

He rang Walworth and after a long puzzling wait the night-watchman answered: site closed, there had been an accident.

'Who are you?'

'The Catholic Church,' Nally said. 'Am I too late?'

'Dead before he knew it, Father.'

There was a great deal of respect now at this close encounter with the annointed. The nightwatchman was pissed.

'May the Lord have mercy on his soul.'

'Amen, Father.'

Nally listened, said compassionate things, was patient, completed the picture.

'God bless you,' he told the nightwatchman and hung up.

He knew precisely what he would wear now: a cheap sombreness would be the motif: dark grey suit, black overcoat, black tie. The hat and spectacles would be important. He chose a Homburg, an offensive brown and jaunty, and rimless reading spectacles perched low so that he could look over them. The effect was cheapness; sharpness too. Tanner a week insurance men had created the image long ago when he was a boy. Then he rang the caretaker at Archway. 'I'm coming down to see you. Be there.' Finally, he took an empty attaché case.

He doffed the hat and spectacles, to carry them; put a Webley pistol in his overcoat pocket, and made his exit to the car park. His car was ready, cleaned of snow, the glass defrosted.

Around him was a fairytale picture: snow-piped winter trees, charcoal branches spiked at the sky; and, below and beyond, the white muffled stillness of the city.

He stood and pondered it a little while and then drove slowly downhill towards Archway. The snow had lessened to lonely drifting motes; the roads and pavements would be a frozen mess soon in the sudden whips of north-east wind.

He parked two blocks away and walked the rest along the almost desolate streets. This birthplace of suburbia was a long-deserted shrine. And then he was among the down-at-heel shops again, the strange transfusion of Carib and Greek and Paki into dry cracking arteries.

Entering the house unobtrusively presented only a slight problem: staying on the near pavement he would present no face to the upstairs windows. But Maisie's ground-floor window, above the area, was a full frontal, Hobson's choice.

Schoolchildren were escaping in black smudges from the red-brick high-rise academies of ailing Victoria; he watched the cringers, the hobblers, the hooligans, and chose his men: three overfed piglets and watched appreciatively the coarseness of horseplay, listened to the shouts of liberated filth. He called them, took a pound coin from his pocket.

'Who's your leader?'

All three answered at once.

'Good.'

He explained his battle plan, a practical joke of course, on a fragile friend: load up with missiles and attack a ground-floor window and then – very important! – re-arm from the front door and basement steps and sustain the onslaught. In, out! He found a fifty pence coin to augment the pound and simplify the sharing. He examined them on strategy, adherence to instructions, praised them in high humour. Very good.

They were off!

He was pleased with them: they were very effective: a rain of snow against the window, exploding, sticking, slipping. And, at the moment of their flight, he had reached the basement door and tapped.

The caretaker, in strict deference, held herself erect as possible as he stepped in. 'Schoolchildren is animals now,' she said.

The rod, the cat, thumb-screws, National Service, Nally agreed. 'Any problems?' he asked, setting a quiet tone.

'Can't think of none,' she told him.

Nally said, 'The place needs a little attention, doesn't it? I'll take a look above. Any changes?'

No changes. 'Still that pair on the top,' she said. 'And the hoor with the fiddle overhead me. One of 'em knocks her off regular. The fucking noise!'

'Part of the business, I'm afraid,' Nally said; he noted the wine bottle and wondered how soon honesty would be eroded.

An afternoon film of thirties dudes and beauties was unfolding on the box; he turned the sound up to the unbearable maximum. 'Leave it like that until I'm up there,' he told her. He stared at her, left her in no doubt.

'Yes,' she said.

Soundlessly, in the storm, two steps at a time, he made the ascent. The blast of distortion faded. The room on the left: a cave would have been more civilised, he thought. From the landing, he saw the pile of damp mouldering refuse in the corner, and listened.

Down below, the hall door opened, a voice, voices, bolts, keys unlocking. That would the 'the hoor with the fiddle'. But there was another voice. A little warmth of anticipation was almost raised to excitement. He would bide a while.

He donned hat and glasses, went into the room on the right and knew it was Hennessy's. There was a sweeping brush: Hennessy even swept it! The window was clean and curtained; in a boxwood wardrobe there was a minimum of clothes, but surprisingly good, Nally thought; and shirts, socks, underwear in a suitcase beneath his bed. Full marks for trying, but the bare walls and bellied ceiling dehumanised it. Nothing under the pillow or mattress either . . .

He had waited twenty minutes, and would allow another ten, he was thinking, when he heard the faintest movement of stair-tread or banister. It was on the next landing. Half the journey already made, with such care, without a sound! He stood in the lee of Hennessy's wardrobe and could judge the breaches of stillness now because he listened for them. Then there was movement next door. Nally arranged hat and spectacles and moved in.

The girl, in a denim suit, a scarf thrown back, tight dark hair, had a foot on the rubbish pile when she sensed Nally and wheeled. Nally saw her reach for the shoulder-bag and with his open hand he swung and slapped her with such force that she was flung across Kirwan's bed and tumbled on the littered floorboards. He took the bag, looked in it, and put it out of reach.

'Get up,' he said; he jabbed her with his shoe. She stood facing him. In her pocket he found a weapon, a spike, short and sharp like a brad-awl. He put it in her bag.

'Looking for something, are we?' he said.

She was a looker, Nally thought, with a good body and limbs; but hard as flint, bitter; a faggot, more than likely; a great waste. Her face was wealed and water ran down from the grey painless eyes. He caught her by the hair, twisted her like a sack and bounced her against the wall. He beat her on the arms and ribs until he could see her lips trembling. Then suddenly he drove a fist into the soft flesh of her stomach, emptied her of air, left her gawping. And then again. She slid down to her knees, dry-retching, hands clenched.

Nally rested against the door jamb for minutes, watched her recovering. Then he lifted her by the scruff, sat her on the bed where she could watch him.

'Hennessy? You were going to cross him, were you? Or meet him, eh?' Nally laughed. 'A heavy-duty crowbar might just about tickle you, you clever sow. Or a navvy's punner.' He scattered the rubbish with his foot, sent maggots, wood-lice, in a panic for darkness. He brought the parcel and laid it on her knees.

'Open it.'

On one side she holed and pulled away the wrapping paper, exposed the neat bundles of tens and twenties. Nally counted it into his attaché case.

'Forty-two thousand. Agreed. An honourable man. That's half. Now, where's the other half?'

She stared at him; her face was swelling, a smear of blood showing at the corner of her mouth.

Nally told her. 'We're not part-timers, are we? I don't think

128

so. We look after number one. You could call us full-time black-hearted villains, eh?'

A little glimmer of interest showed for a moment.

'You're in a tough spot,' he said. 'I'll beat you till you're in twilight. Leave you for the Law. They'll be hard on you, you're special. The whole bag of tricks, slops and screw-sucking till your teeth fall out. Rotten prognosis.' He slapped her, not at all gently, on the cheek. 'It's make your mind up time.'

She nodded.

'Good.'

'You mean you'd cross the Law?' she said.

Nally said, 'Exclude the Law.'

'What do I get?'

'A headstart. If you're lucky. Where's the other half?'

'A guess.'

Nally waited.

'With Hennessy.'

'Good. You want a headstart. I want Hennessy.' Nally stood and listened for a moment, held up a hand for silence, cautiously closed the door to a slim crack of light, spoke softly. 'Hennessy is dust in the wind, that's all. It won't worry you to trade him, will it?'

'No.'

'Sometimes the Law is an ass, just for the bat of an eyelid. That's the time.' He stood, listening, whispered, 'I want the other half. Understand?'

'Yes.'

'The other parcel. The Law looks after itself. Hennessy is a paddy-joke and slime like you are nothing at all. I want the loot. Mine. Tomorrow you can play cops and bombers again. Maybe. But say your piece now. Very quiet.'

'He'll ring.'

'Hennessy?'

'Yes.'

'You'd wait for him, you said?'

'Yes.'

Nally's whisper faded away: he stood still, just in the shade of the door. Traffic in the street seemed remote as if the white day had blotted up all sound; bus wheels made a blunted track in the roadway slurry. It was growing dark. The girl sat motionless on the bed, watching him, cold as the bare icy room, the curtainless window. Nally could smell the rotting clothes and leather he had disturbed; he remembered the squirm of pale maggots and the fragile beauty of Helena and his stone house looking down the hill. Later, they might stand together, well wrapped and padded, and watch the Guy Fawkes evening shooting up from council parks, dingy gardens, vacant lots. It might be a good night for fireworks yet: a clear gelid sky and wind to put smoke and gunge to flight. He could hear the gauche creeping footsteps on the stairs plainly now. The girl listened too. Nally knew she was in pain, sore where he had hammered chest and arms and shoulders; a ridge of tightening ache in her guts.

He crossed, stood her at the bed, gathered Kirwan's discarded clothes from the floor, put his case on the bed, took his place beside her. They were facing the door.

The footsteps were on the landing now; a board creaked; sounds came from Hennessy's room: the click of the wardrobe latch, the drag of the suitcase from under the bed. Ten minutes, longer, very thorough.

Nally arranged spectacles and hat, nodded to the girl to tidy up; with a handkerchief and saliva he gently cleaned the blood from her mouth.

Suddenly the door was open and Cleary stood there. The instant materialisation of the figures facing him, the ragged bed, the attaché case, seemed to slap him with shock. Strange faces. For a moment he was poised for flight.

Nally said in a small deferential voice, 'Afternoon, guv'nor. I represent the funeral furnishers. My assistant.' The girl nodded. 'A relative, are you? My condolences.'

A wave of relief swept over Cleary. Coming, sour, empty-handed, from Hennessy's room, he had blundered in and stood helpless, fighting against panic.

'You went in the wrong room,' Nally said. 'We heard you rummaging about but didn't like to interfere.'

All the poison and frustration of Cleary's day gathered for

spitting. 'Searching the room, are you? Is that usual?'

'There are occasions, guv'nor.'

'My name is Cleary,' he said. 'Transport Manager.'

'Ah, sorry, guv'nor.'

'Officially here.' Cleary stared at Nally's garb, the mourning bits, the currying reverential face. 'In connection with the accident, you understand?'

'Of course.'

'Do you search clothes, look into pockets, under mattresses as a matter of routine?'

'There are occasions,' Nally began.

'You said that before.'

'To establish identity.'

'His name was Kirwan.'

Nally glanced at the girl for reaction: not a movement, not an amateur twitch. 'Ah, that settles it,' he said gratefully. 'And of course items can be left in rooms, in pockets, personal items, that might be distressful to those who are grieving.' Nally had produced a notebook and pencil. 'Kirwan, you said. Spelling?'

'No idea!' Cleary snapped at him.

'And you are Mr Cleary.'

'My name is not relevant.' Cleary stared at him and thought there might be the suspicion of a smile in Nally's respectful glance. 'But yours is!' he said. 'Who are you?'

Nally took a page from his book and wrote a meaningless name and telephone number. 'That's my guv'nor. He'll fill you in. My name's Percy Jinks.'

An arse-licking corpse-blocker, Cleary thought, with his suitcase and apparatus. But he was safe, moving now: behind him a bridge or two burned, the future uncharted. But in motion.

He said outrageously to Nally, 'I suppose there are thieves in every trade. Cocks and hens.' He looked with undisguised contempt at them both and hurried away.

From the landing, Nally called after him, 'Sorry if we upset you, guv'nor. Just doing our job.'

Nally came back and stood at the window. He said to the girl, 'Leave your bag. I'll know you won't get jiggy.' He patted the bulk of his own pocket. 'At the time of speaking I'm your best friend, remember.'

'Yes.'

'You knew Kirwan, did you?'

'I met him this morning.'

'Of course.' Nally thought about it. 'Yes, he's dead. An accident, I'm told. Our man, Hennessy, knocked something over. A ton weight, twenty foot drop.' He watched her. 'Is it important?'

'No.'

'Good.'

Down below the hall door slammed on the bare frustration of Cleary. The girl listened for sounds of Maisie but there was nothing.

Nally gazed down on the pavements for Cleary and saw him emerge: the pale ravaged self-abused face, dead hair, a staleness, black-edged overgrown nails, small eyes: begrudging, vicious, Nally thought. He watched him on the pavements: a kind of scurrying run, and from the corner a fearful backward glance; like a rabbit, he sensed danger. And well he might, Nally thought. He took his attaché case, looked at his watch, steered the girl to the landing and stairway.

'Kirwan's woman is at home,' she said. 'She doesn't know.'

'Ah!' Nally smiled. 'Then we'll be very quiet.'

The caretaker looked at the calendar on the wall: she couldn't remember if she had bought it sometime in drunkenness, or found it perhaps, or pinched it. She used to pinch liquor in the offies once but the Pakis had them now and train-robbers would think twice. She would have found the calendar, she decided; it wasn't worth pinching. She looked at the month – June! – and was startled. She counted on her fingers: four, five months gone like a nod-off in a chair. The wine in bottle and blood was spent; she let drops gather and fall into her empty glass. It had been a hot June, she remembered, airless in her single basement room: she used to sleep in her gross pendulous nakedness. Nally gave her free lodging; she collected his rents and got cash, a few pounds in her hand. Her pension too. She could afford to drink a bit; food didn't matter a lot.

The room had a junk-shop smell and pattern, with access from door to door, table space in the middle, and the fringes piled high; her bed was almost hidden behind a mirrored what-not, stacked chairs, a fridge, a sewing machine. A picture of a smiling dodgy man hung on a salvaged space of wall; he had a crooked winsome grin. He had been dead four years and she had brought a lifetime's chattels with her to come and work for Nally.

Nally found her in this toppling Rembrandt study, bottle poised over glass, the day's grey-soiled light never reaching a high-point. He had been standing moments, watching, before her eyes focused him and she made a startled flatulent noise that might have eructed from either extremity.

'Granted,' Nally said in colloquial humour. He brought the girl from behind him and displayed her.

'Dear Christ!' the caretaker said. 'You came in like a ghost! Of a sudden I felt there's something ... someone ...' She emitted another clappered gush of noise, waved her hand to disperse panic and pong, and finally, with a spray-can sent prodigal clouds of aerosol lavender into suspense.

'I should leave it,' Nally advised her.

She looked at the listed fragrance on the tin. 'I don't like it none either,' she said. 'Sweet, ain't it, like a hoor's funeral?'

'I haven't had the pleasure,' Nally said, but she missed it.

'Tea?'

'Oh, we're fine,' Nally told her; he saw the bottle and glass and even the struggling light shone through the emptiness of both. 'Why don't you have a drink?'

'I never do, very much, till evening time.'

Nally looked at the bottle.

'Just the odd bottle at home when I'm feeling down. Home drinking is bad, you know?'

'It's dark now,' Nally said, looking out. 'Early for the pubs, is it?'

She made a little spitting noise of amusement. 'Round here

it's in at the back and rap. Irish, you know. Thick as planks, most of 'em.'

'Yes,' Nally said in sympathy; he gave her a fiver. 'Comfortable, are they?'

'Good fires in the pubs, give 'em credit.'

'Take an hour,' Nally said. 'Have a nip and a heat, good for the feet.'

She looked at the girl, wondered how she had arrived. Had Nally let her in at the hallway? Had he given her one upstairs? Was he here for another one? She looked knackered already. She wondered and worried. 'The bed's not great,' she said. 'Didn't do me linen this week. The weather, busy too, you see . . .'

'Don't worry,' Nally said. 'We'll manage on our feet.'

His smile hurried her into her coat and shapeless hat. As she made her exit he put two pounds on the table. 'A bottle of plonk for later.'

Another happy day: her face shone at Nally. She was gone. A single bar of a heater glowed, the television glimmered like a candle.

A few moments of silence. Nally looked at the battered lumber of a lifetime, the picture-face smiling because he had left it all behind. He watched the ceiling, listened.

He said, 'Was she drunk up there? Kirwan's piece?'

'Not used to drinking.'

'Flat out?'

'The slam of the door didn't wake her.'

He remembered Cleary's slamming exit and nodded. Cleary hovered in his mind like the bad smell of the room: there had been something in the manner of Cleary's vengeful comic retreat and the cheap sneer of thievery that rankled. Thievery was for tea-leaves. The wise were just wicked enough, Nally thought, in a wicked world; students of battle, retreat, tricks, ubiquity . . .

A small dangerous bastard, Cleary; McLeod had him listed, of course, but a little scourging could only chasten him for the solitude ahead.

Nally looked at his watch. 'Will Hennessy ring, you think?'

'Yes.'

'No doubt?'

'No.'

He smiled at her confidence, at the easy push-door she had found to Hennessy's kindness; he guided her out, sat her on the small rise of stairs to the telephone landing where he could watch her. 'Sit.' He could see the pain as she bent, eyes moist with anger.

There was a call to be made: it would be untimely, a trifle luckless at any rate, if it clashed with Hennessy's. But time was precious; and Hennessy was in pledge to the steely clever tramp at his feet. He took out coins and dialled Walworth and wondered if Feehan might answer. But it was the nightwatchman again.

'I know your voice,' he said, drunker now but sharp as a tack. 'You're the Catholic Church.'

'Excellent,' Nally said. 'I wanted to speak with Mr Feehan about the Requiem Mass.'

'Gone for hours. The driver took him home.'

'The driver took him home? Mr Feehan? Not unwell, I hope.'

'Must have run at a brick wall last night, Father, his face is a busted jam-jar. Then all the blood and brains here this morning ... you see ...'

'Of course, of course. And the driver took him home? The driver who had the accident?'

'That's it, Father.'

Nally clicked out with his finger and dialled Paddington.

Feehan answered: he had been asleep, Nally knew. 'I meant to ring you,' Feehan said. 'There was an accident ...'

'Yes, yes, I know,' Nally said. 'We can talk about it later on. How are you feeling now?'

'All right,' Feehan said.

'You were cut up last night?'

'A bit.'

'At Cricklewood?'

'Yes.'

'Hennessy?'

'Yes.'

'Don't worry about the accident,' Nally said. 'The night-watchman told me. You were guiding him in?'

'Yes.'

An accident? Now there's a thing, Nally thought: it hadn't struck him before. 'Bad driving, nothing else.' He pronounced in favour of the guilty. 'I want you to do something for me. Are you well enough?'

'Oh yes.'

'It might take a couple of hours or more.'

'That's all right.'

'There's a little clerk at Haringey ...' Nally painted an unpleasant picture. 'Nosey ... vindictive ... dangerous. Have you got it?'

'Cleary,' Feehan said.

'The very man. A friend of Hennessy's. He's making accident inquiries.' Nally waited seconds for a response.

'Inquiries?'

'Trying to shift the blame, I'd say.' Nally sighed impatience. 'I've told Bredin to haul him off, of course. But he could make a statement to the Law.'

The girl, still and listening, moved a little in pain, made a small sound. Nally kicked her in warning.

Eventually Feehan said, 'What should I do?'

'Be very hard.'

'Yes.'

'Very, very hard, you understand? Get over to Highbury, park, wait for him.' Nally somehow didn't care to remember McLeod's door number, only the road. 'He's on his way there now. You could beat him to it.'

'Wait for him?'

'Ten minutes only. Then move to Turnpike.' It was a wild fling: he gave him Bredin's address. 'Spend an hour there.'

'My car,' Feehan said. 'Hennessy nicked it.'

'Oh yes,' Nally remembered. 'He drove you home.'

There was silence.

'Didn't he?'

'He dumped me at Hoxton,' Feehan said. 'Pulled away. Left a gun in my pocket. I was almost out.' Feehan might be close to whatever savage tears he could shed. 'I'm not long at Paddington.'

'Keep the gun for me. You're fit, are you?'

'Yes.'

'Take minicabs as you go, right? We'll talk about Hennessy later. Move now, make a shift! And you'll be careful, of course.'

Nally hung up, waited in silence for ten, fifteen minutes. The television sound track of the long-ago film, the creaking music of suspense, the schmaltz of sainted violins, crept and gushed from the basement; the unmistakable voices, dead as dust, played their own tune of quirks and mannerisms. The caretaker should have switched it off; Nally was paying the bills. He would keep it in mind. He looked down at the girl.

'When Hennessy rings,' he said suddenly. 'Too bad if he doesn't. He's your best trump. Only trump. You need goods to go to market.' He prodded her with his foot. 'Speak up. Join the party.'

'Yes?'

'He's coming here?'

'I don't know.'

'But you think so?'

'Yes.'

Nally thought about it. Fouling one's own doorstep was never a recommended tactic. Violence, mayhem on the streets, had a certain transience, like a pond: a splash, a ripple and calm. Always splashes out there, here, there, everywhere. But houses, door numbers, gave locus and significance.

'You'll discourage him. Put him off. Describe Cleary for him. Tell him he's out there in the snow, smelling about. You're worried, you see? Another place. A street, a corner, somewhere in the back-doubles.'

'Where?'

'Hennessy will know. You want the time and the place, that's all. Understand?'

'Yes.'

Nally looked at his watch: he would wait ten minutes, no more. Hennessy might have dummied, wrong-footed them all: Feehan, Kirwan, the girl, Nally. When the die was cast

Hennessy would be clever enough to run. The cameras at Paddington would have smelt of Law and that would be starter's orders . . .

The television track crept in again. Nally remembered the films, the handsome square-jawed heroes, the cast-iron dialogue, Saturday matinées, the wartime streets outside; he remembered doorsteps painted red, little doors, little hallways, little rooms, dungarees drying out at weekends. Such pride in survival, skimping, going without, setting aside the burial sums at a tanner a week. And then he thought of Hennessy and the girl again . . .

The telephone rang. Nally booted her, watched the pain of straightening up and walking. He stood behind her, clamped his arms about her, shared the earpiece.

'Yes?' she said.

'This is Hennessy.'

'Are you all right?' Nally listened to the solicitude flowing out from her and knew the eyes would be cold motionless alleys. 'I was worried for you.'

'There was an accident. I'm moving now.'

'Where are you?'

'The Boro, London Bridge. Archway in an hour, maybe more, maybe less. When I can.'

Nally prodded her.

'No, not here! There's someone out there.'

'Watching?'

'Two hours shuffling about in doorways.'

'That's Cleary.'

'Small, pale, dirty.'

'You can get past him!'

'Oh yes, easy. But you?'

'Listen.'

'Yes?'

'Off the Cally for Liverpool Road there's an open space, a pub.' He gave her the name. 'A bonfire built up, ready for the touch. Big. And a phone box. The pub's the marker.'

'A bus number?'

'Not a bus route. Get a spade driver, he'll know it.' Hennessy gave her time and place. 'Hour and a half, two, give or take, I'll be there. Lose yourself in the dark, watch the phone box.'

'Is there something I should bring for you?'

'No,' Hennessy said.

Nally nodded, smiled humourlessly.

'You have everything?'

'Everything.'

She paused a moment or two. 'I owe you,' she said. 'You've done a good job.'

Nally smiled again, wondered if there hadn't been a thread of sincerity in it.

'Be there,' Hennessy said. 'You have a long road. And there's something else.'

'Yes.'

'Kirwan's dead.'

Nally watched her stand in silence, long dragging seconds, until Hennessy spoke again.

'Are you all right?'

'Yes.'

'There was an accident.'

'Oh God!' she said.

Nally's admiration swelled, and his wariness too.

Hennessy was asking again, 'Are you all right?' And the wealed face was quiet, composed as a plaster image.

'Are you all right?'

'Yes.' This time, a whisper only.

'I'm sorry,' Hennessy said.

Another long pause before she said, 'I'm all right now.'

'You'll tell Maisie?'

'Yes.'

'Be careful.'

'Yes.'

Nally took the phone gently from her hand and replaced it. With a sudden short kick at her heels he up-ended her and she fell like a sack, sprawled, groaning in pain.

'You're a dangerous cow,' he said. 'But I suppose a bargain is a bargain.'

He dialled McLeod's number.

'Yes.' McLeod answered at once.

'I'm at Euston,' Nally said. 'Our girl bought a ticket for Manchester. Just now. Same whore's rig as last night. Blonde and cheap . . .'

McLeod had hung up: at his black phone he would be sending out his terriers for the kill.

'On your feet,' Nally told her.

She stood facing him. He gave her two hundred pounds. 'I'd visit distant friends if I were you.' He altered and arranged himself with care, locked the attaché case, checked the Webley. 'I don't ever want to see you again. Remember that.' He descended the little steps to the basement, moved out of sight.

There was a huge silence when he switched off the box on his way and hardly a sound as he pulled the street door behind him.

She waited perhaps thirty seconds and began the laborious climb to Kirwan's room. Even half a lungful of air sent pain shooting off to complete a circuit and she held her arms tight about her chest for relief. Her ribs were bruised, cracked maybe. Heat throbbed in her face, in her mind.

Her bag was in Kirwan's room; she put it on her shoulder again, studied it, took a mirror and examined her face, rubbed a line of dried blood from the hidden curves of her lips, arranged her hair. There was a style of pace and movement, she found, where the level of pain was acceptable. She went quietly downstairs and stood at Maisie's door. It was an irritating, seemingly purposeless duty but she had measured pros and cons and found a shade of advantage in leaving confusion and incoherence behind her.

She knocked, pushed open the door and roused Maisie from the torpor of her lunchtime bender.

'Jesus!' Maisie shouted. 'The door!' She was on her feet.

The girl closed it, put a finger to lip for silence. 'He rang. Hennessy rang.'

Bemused, dry-mouthed, Maisie groped, fumbled at putting pieces together. 'He rang?' Her strange fairytale day was taking shape again and she was laughing. 'Oh God, my head! Where are they? He rang? I never heard the phone, not a sound.'

'I'm going to meet Hennessy.'

'Christ!' Maisie said. 'My coat, my wedding coat creased!'
She felt for the reassurance of her outrageous hat and tilted it.
'My coat, out of the shop and creased!' She took a bottle of
whiskey from the debris of her shopping spree and put it with
glasses on a table. 'For Bill,' she said.

The girl waited for an adequate silence and said, 'Kirwan is
dead.'

She took the bottle of whiskey from the table and drank the
scalding unpleasantness of it for her own pummelled flesh, and
put the bottle in Maisie's hand.

'A site accident,' she said, flat and hard. 'Dead.'

The telephone was ringing on the basement landing. 'It'll be
for you, I think.'

'For me?' Maisie asked.

'Yes.'

Maisie walked past, seemingly brisk and impatient, glancing
a bewilderment and compassion as at the discovery of a fatal
imbalance in someone cherished, almost loved. She saw only
the eyes, cold as madness.

'Yes,' she was saying at the phone. 'That's my name.'

The girl moved away as fast as pain and breath would allow.
She gave ten pounds to the Greek mini-driver across the way
and told him, 'Drive round a while. Plenty of time. Be sure
you're not followed. Very sure.'

He looked at the shiny bruise on her cheek-bone, the flushed
finger-weals, and nodded. For half an hour he wove a haphazard pattern in the grim white almost deserted back-streets,
hither, thither, the long, the short.

'Nothing,' he said.

She gave him Hennessy's marker – the pub, the phone box –
and in the same zigzag whimsy he took a long time to reach it.
'Good luck,' he offered and a wink of camaraderie for the
pursued. He left her expertly in the deep shadows between
distant kerb lights.

There was a junction of three forgotten streets, the pub's dim
glimmer like a sparkle in the wilderness. The phone box was a
glimmer too, aerosoled in spews of cellulose and, behind it, an
acre of weeds and rubble that wartime's affluence could afford

to scarify but beyond the poverty of peacetime to restore.

The bonfire was a towering mound of waste, spent furniture, bedding, whatever was portable and combustible. The white mat of snow was trampled with comings and goings at its perimeter.

As she paused, a youth set aflame a soaked rag corked in a bottle of spirit and there was a cheer when he aimed it and pitched it in a long fluttering arc. It shattered in an explosion of flame and brought memories of other littered streets and waste-land. She watched where the wind carried the smoke – and would carry the heat soon – and went towards houses, small, boarded, violated, perishing; and at an extremity, a single squat or doss with sacking on a window. She found a shell of room and bay window and built a seat in the darkness. There was no glass; the smoke swirled in, escaped through a gap of doorway.

She thought momentarily of Kirwan and Maisie and Hennessy. She groaned with her own pain. There was a night to be spent in cover, buried, to let the eagerness of searchers cool: at night-time shadows were substance, footfalls like thunderclaps. In the first light, with people and traffic in a new day, she would move. In a half-dozen suburbs there were sleeping cars and she had keys for all of them. She would go south for the coast. A holiday with distant friends; a holiday from pain, she thought.

She had come too, she knew, to watch Nally in the tidying up of his business. Her body was sore where he had hammered it, her arms; a tighening ache of muscle in her stomach. She remembered the jarring of spine and teeth when he had kicked her feet out and she had fallen like a stone. He was a vicious dangerous animal; civilised, murderous too if ever there was the need. Beside him, Hennessy was a poor threadbare teeter-ing joke. Hennessy was second-hand cars, Sunday booze, paddles in the sea, morals like gobstoppers in a bag, come-day-go-day till death do us part. Nally was an aboriginal savage, every day his enemy. You needed to be that hard.

Cleary had slammed the street door and as the spear of wind caught him, his littleness, an empty-handed exit into the awful hostile world, had even more sharpness to pierce him. Nally's words of what seemed only moments before, sent obsequiously to him on the stairs, had an unpleasant after-taste of gibe. 'Sorry if we upset you, guv'nor. Just doing our job.' The retreating eyes, busy hands, the girl's discoloured face, lifeless. Corpse-washers! He thought of his terror and loathing of Bredin, the awful reeling illness and the vomit at his feet; the ugliness of machinery, the dirt-embedded hands of fitters. 'Ha, ha! you wanker!'

The wind came with a dry edge along the pavements, nailing down snow and footprints, bleaching skin, flapping the tarpaulin rags on a corner news-stand; on a clear patch of pavement it froze the trickles of water from a fish shop arcade into tangled strings of ice. In the sky above Highgate a Guy Fawkes rocket burst and then another. But Cleary didn't see them as he trotted from the side-streets to the bustle of Holloway and Seven Sisters. At Finsbury Park station he was tiring; the wind struck him at the vortex of so many streets and he groaned before the sharpness of it. It had weeded the world of people, he thought, until only the dirty brickwork of houses was left pointing up at the growing darkness. In the grip of impotence and longing he remembered the office, the gas heat that he could almost feel flowing out from the grill of the radiator to circle him with sleep.

He was sick with weariness. Disillusionment, like cold, soaked deadeningly into his mind. He crossed the street to the station approach. He would take a bus down close to Clissold Park, only minutes to McLeod's door, his bedroom, the warmth, the world locked outside.

But as he reached the bus stop, the pavements, the last drop of his anger fell away and fear, stealthily as a stroke, overwhelmed him: a terrifying breathless confusion and when it had passed he was shorn of resistance; panic was an abrading thread exposed in his mind.

He remembered Nally and the girl again; and Nally's eyes, the fleshy face. The girl? A charade, he thought, and tried to remember flaws in the performances but there were none. That was the danger, and it came in one flickering second of presentiment.

He fought the last battle with himself, groping about for the cleverness of plans, but the sharpness of insecurity obtruded, distracted him. In the bleak windswept streets the hunt had already swung about and he was the quarry. Inexplicably he knew it. Kirwan had died down at the foot of a tunnel shaft and only Hennessy or Feehan might have killed him. And he knew with a deep illogical certainty that it was Feehan. And somewhere lay the money; and the smiling corpse-washer and the girl were in it too . . .

'Jesus help me!' he said aloud like a prayer.

From the bus stop he gazed into the High Road as if somehow forewarning might signal to him like a pin-prick beacon from the mixing pattern of scampering people.

McLeod. He would turn back to the security of heavy doors, solid walls, where he was the observer. It was a moment of hope. The day seemed to crystallise and chip away in the last rush of spent commuters grinding the pavements: some comfort in each frozen mind sustained them. He would unburden himself to McLeod, give him everything – no tricks, no hidden aces – and there would be safety . . .

A stationary bus at the terminus came to life and moved across to the queue where he stood and they shuffled aboard. He sat nearest the door, there somehow closer to home, impervious of dripping platform, swirling draughts. They crossed Seven Sisters and gathered speed along the polyglot world of Blackstock Road: he tightened his watered eyes and dabbed at them with his coat sleeve.

He looked back. The pavements were dirty white fringes for the highway of slush, frozen now and cracking. And behind his bus the wiper-blades of a car, black spastic metronomes, pushed back the filthy spray and snow-motes dry as flour. In the passenger seat, behind the clear segment of glass, he saw a bandaged face craning forward, peering up at him. And then he saw the hat.

It was Feehan!

He looked about him in terror: reasons, plots, loot, shrunk to insignificance. Only escape was important. The bus, in a string of traffic, moved at a fair pace, and Cleary jumped, hands outstretched like a crashing footballer, for the kerb. Someone shouted and he fell across the refuse bins of a café, stumbled on past blurred shapes and images, and found deliverance in a side street. The bus would have slowed and stopped, he knew. And Feehan's cab. Only his awful fear gave him the strength to keep moving; and he was on the home ground of familiar turns and land-marks. For fifteen minutes he ran, trotted, hid in door-ways for breath, and searched the empty convergences behind him. He seemed to have won, broken free. From his cover he could see McLeod's tall prestigious house in the near distance, its bulk, lights in windows, refuge. He would be in the warmth of a bed with soft light falling on eiderdown and linen and feel an almost holy safeness in the friendly things about him. It beckoned with the enchantment of a schoolboy's dream ...

He began to move again and, at once, the warm dream, the reassurance, the safety vanished. He saw a distant movement from light into shadow and the pale grey hat flicked in and out of vision.

The dread that took possession of him now was total and he fled, half crying, from street to street, darkness to darkness. It began to snow again, tiny wafting specks, like swarms in the darkness, falling down on the slush of the world. A tall famished church emerged from billowing curtains of white, advertised like a trader, 'God is at your service, are you at His?', and a loose corner of the coloured poster flapped in despair. Cleary stood and watched it and the snow burned against his face, blotted out with bitterness the square stony importance of heaven: a score of gods had come to suspire in our midst and hurried back to their lush armchairs again; he needed one to stay below, take rooms with him where he could learn the tricks of salvation. There hadn't been any gods for a long time.

His legs were failing. He peered, listened, stumbled into the darkness of an abandoned mews. He lay flat on the ground, exhausted.

He might have lain a half an hour, he thought, recovering, almost as if consciousness were returning to him with the small faraway sounds of the evening, the bite of frost, the discomfort of the lumpy ground beneath him. The sweat had seeped out hot from his body and began to grow cold on his skin. He got to his feet, remained standing in the darkness: had he awakened there in the chillness of the evening remembering pieces of a dream? It was like groping back for some febrile memory of awareness.

He listened. Traffic sounded somewhere in the distance and he aimed himself towards it, stiff in his legs now, feeling the chill dampness of his clothes. Disorientation, plodding on without purpose or direction, was triggering panic again; his pulse quickened, raced out of control. At every convergence there was a scurrying figure and the certainty of danger in isolation; and, back on peopled streets again, there was the uncertainty of safety in changing crowds and traffic movement.

He skirted a hospital, hurried by the casualty entrance: a sloping ramp, a tiled corridor, a glimpse of pillows, cylinders, a red blanket, a glittering trolley. If they murdered him like Kirwan, he thought, his body perhaps threaded to consciousness would be rolled along the bright passages and he would know the smell of ether coming close to his face, the rapid clanging echoes of his mind, the whirl of pictures and no more. How long did it take to die? When breathing stopped and limp hands were folded across did the pain go on inside the shell? He leant back against iron railings for breath, searched the sparse crowds for Feehan. But it might not be Feehan, it might be anyone. Feehan might stand with infinite patience by McLeod's doorstep and somewhere out there a faceless surrogate stalked, watched. Cleary examined pinched hurrying faces. There was an Underground at Manor House only a little way off, and he thought that if with caution he went down and waited until only a few faces were left with him, he could be sure. He could wait until the doors were rumbling and make the sudden rush. But if he were caught there alone? ...

He stood almost resignedly at the railings while time slipped past, afraid to move, shivering with cold, and then at once, miraculously again, everything was patent, blindingly simple. A taxi, its red plying light a beam of salvation, moved towards him and he flagged it down. They would wait for him at Highbury, that was the trap.

'Turnpike,' he told the driver.

Confidence fell on him like a warm shower. Bredin would be home, back from the filthy yard, the desk at the window, and he found his loathing for him lessening before the remembrance of the huge sheltering body, the spread of shoulders, the hoarse bitter voice.

Bredin! Bredin!

Bredin was the great protective loving god with outstretched arms. He sat wearily in the cab. He could garnish and regale for Bredin the hours he had kept going, the danger, the need to harden, to stave off panic. Payment for Bredin.

The taxi went through West Green Road, past junk stores and bogus pool clubs where Mediterraneans in dandy clothes, effeminate whirls of hair, seemed weary of dilettantism. London was dying.

He watched the evening with growing contentment. Had he ever been pursued or afraid? Fireworks popped, exploded like gunshots in the streets. He remembered the phone box at Bredin's corner where he could ring McLeod. Everything fell in place, dove-tailed. He would be clipped, low-key, even blunt with McLeod. That would be the style.

At Turnpike he paid the taxi, waited and could find no discord in streams of traffic or people to disturb his contentment. Then he hurried along through the frozen hinterland until he saw the phone box and behind it the piled scrap-yard and crane jib draped in snow.

He rang McLeod.

'Where are you?'

'Turnpike.'

'Ah?'

'Very busy too. You'll be interested.'

'Good. You're coming now?'

'I'm locked out, you see.'

'Are you?'

'There's a watchdog at your door. Bandaged face, grey hat.'

There was silence.

Eventually McLeod said, 'I'll handle this end.'

'Could be dangerous.'

'An hour or so, I'll send a taxi for you. All right?'

'Fine.' He gave him Bredin's address.

Cleary hung up, stood on the pavement and smiled at the bitter wickedness of the night. The final neatness of the package surprised and delighted him. He moved on, paused to look up at the light shining from Bredin's room.

There was a disused basement in the house with iron railings and six stone steps leading to what had been a servants' entrance.

Feehan came up noiselessly out of the darkness. A hundred yards away someone had come out from a hallway: a slamming door, harsh nicotine cough and spit, steel tips hammering through the slush of pavements; there was the sound of a car not very far off. Feehan moved out, crouched and brought his whole weight in a swinging jab to Cleary's stomach. The little hunched body toppled against him. He lifted him down into the darkness of the basement. The car passed, the steel tips came and grew distant and less urgent.

Cleary groaned in the agony of breathlessness and Feehan waited, held him erect, until he saw consciousness and then fear coming into his eyes.

'I'm going to give you a chance to be very brave,' he said. 'I'm going to beat you senseless and I don't want you to make a sound while I'm doing it.'

Cleary's pale, dirty hands stretched out, pleading.

'But if you make a sound I'll kill you.'

'Feehan!' Cleary said. 'Oh Christ, Feehan . . .'

Feehan reached over to him with Hennessy's gun, put the muzzle against his chin. 'If I pull the trigger now,' he said, 'I'll blow out your teeth, the top of your bastard head.'

Cleary was trembling, the sweat seemed suddenly to be painted across his face.

'So don't make a sound.'

Feehan put the gun in his pocket and commenced: it took less than five minutes to pummel and blind the consciousness in Cleary's mind and then he went on beating him for ten, fifteen minutes, until he was weary of it: he had beaten the face into shapelessness and battered head, ribs, groin, wherever the blows fell, until exhaustion slowed and halted him. He left Cleary sprawled, face downwards, on a drift of virgin snow and went away.

A half-hour later Bredin thought he heard from the hallway the rattle of the letter box. He found Cleary. Blood smeared the door where he had clawed at it. He pulled him into the light. There was no face only raw bleeding flesh gashed deep where the bone had jutted beneath it: the lips were split and horrible, slopping across broken teeth and gums.

Bredin left sickness hovering in his mind and then an uncontrollable manic anger took possession of him.

He rang for an ambulance, watched it drive away into the darkness with Cleary, the blue roof-lights signalling frantically back to him from the distance, and as he climbed the stairs to his room, framing Hennessy in his mind, the wailing hee-haw of the siren was still in his ears.

He knelt and opened his suitcase, took out a gun wrapped in stiff dusty oil-rags.

Helena fussed about Nally: how prodigal with health and wind and limb he was, generous with his time, at everyone's beck and call. He put his attaché case on the bed. When he had showered she brought him warm underwear, casual clothes. In roll-neck sweater, Donegal jacket, charcoal slacks, deep tan brogues, he looked quite handsome. She arranged a pale blue silk handkerchief to peep discreetly from his breast pocket.

'Dashing,' she said.

He kissed her.

'Now you must eat.'

'Later,' he told her with the kind of unmistakable firmness she understood. 'I'll be busy for a couple of hours or more. We might go out and have something special then?'

She stood like a gentle smiling saint at the doorway and winked.

Nally laughed happily so that she would hear it as she went downstairs and be flattered.

He drank a little brandy and relaxed and updated himself. Cleary and the girl: a stroke of fortune that they both should come to him at Archway. Money, of course; bees and the honey pot.

The attaché case was on his bed and beyond the stillness of his room everything was in motion.

The tunneller, the Kirwan fellow at Walworth, had been Feehan's. To Nally, a casualty, a dummy, nothing more. Feehan had arranged punishment, that was the way of it. Savage of course. And now Feehan, with more to conceal than gaucherie and neglect, was in search of Cleary. That also was the way of it. There might be a great thunderbolt of punishment descending on Cleary. It was of little importance: they meddled, let them get on with it. Tonight the boards would be swept clean. Hennessy, Feehan, Cleary, snapped up and away. Immured. The girl? Not strange, it was the hard and blooded went free as air. A cold dangerous bitch, he knew.

Well, Nally thought, McLeod came out well enough, too well at times, in exchange for gathered whispers here and there; he couldn't win all the pots. McLeod was high in Nally's priorities but Nally was on top. And there would always be bombers: one more or less out there was an irrelevance.

He rang McLeod.

'The girl? At Euston? Did you get her?'

'Not yet.' McLeod said. 'We have people on the train. A non-stop, you see.'

'Good. She might do a quick change. Clever, I'd say.'

'Very.'

'I hope she travelled.'

'Always a possibility,' McLeod said.

'I've arranged for Feehan to be at home for you this evening. Later. You'll see to him?'

'And Cleary,' McLeod confirmed; and then he asked 'How's the other one?'

'Very close,' Nally told him; he nodded towards the attaché case as if McLeod were present. 'Half the jackpot here with me now.'

'Good.'

'The other half, our driver friend too, a little later, I hope. I need a couple of hours. I'll ring you.'

'Nice to have a clean slate tomorrow,' McLeod said.

'I'm looking forward to it.'

Nally heard Helena's footsteps from the corridor, a little discretionary tune of forewarning she sometimes sent ahead of her. He rang off, locked the attaché case in the cupboard of his desk.

'Are you in?' she said. 'There's a Mr Bredin to see you.'

'Ah?'

'Big as a buffalo.'

Nally thought about it for moments. 'It's all right,' he said eventually. 'You can bring him.'

He didn't see Bredin often; sometimes a month or two would pass between visits to the yard at Haringey. Bredin was a coarse blunt island of integrity; visits were not snaps of surveillance. Courtesies perhaps, if that were possible.

He thought Bredin looked ill, his colour raging purple high. He greeted him with suitable warmth and seated him.

'You'll have a drink.'

'Who's Hennessy?' Bredin said, skipping the niceties, hard as a battered anvil.

'Hennessy?' Nally said. He brought Bredin a gill of pale malt whiskey in a cut glass tumbler. 'A driver, isn't he? You must know him.'

'I know him,' Bredin said. 'But who is he?'

'A driver. Fairly good, I'm told,' Nally said. 'That's all.' Bredin drank back most of the whiskey. Nally could see his hands were trembling. 'Something wrong, is there?'

Bredin might have said yes or no.

Nally said, 'Can I help?'

'Hennessy. Where is he?'

Behind an adequate mask of concern Nally carefully considered it and chose his course. 'In fact I'm looking for him myself.'

Bredin waited.

'There was an accident at Walworth.'

'An accident!' Bredin said.

Nally ignored it. 'Yes. Some chap killed. I'm making inquiries. These things happen, part of the business. But you see' – Nally paused for emphasis – '. . . Hennessy assaulted Feehan, flattened him, took off in Feehan's car, company's car. We could be in bother if he's a raving drunk loose on the town.' He topped up Bredin's glass.

Bredin said, 'He's a fucking spy!'

Nally stared at him for a long time, wondered where the strange uncharted track was leading: at such times patience was the unfailing compass point, he knew. 'A spy?'

'A peeper, a backyard sentry, A nark! A copper's nark!'

'Surely!' Nally began. He paced to and fro to show his puzzlement, the absurdity. And then he was reconsidering, thinking aloud. 'He's done his share of thieving of course, I know. They all do. Other people's bits and pieces, not mine. I usually hear these things. Probably does a bit with miles and gallons too if he's not watched.' He glanced at Bredin and conceded a little. 'He could be greedy, I suppose. Narking? Yes. A soft touch for the greedy eye, you know.' Nally stopped suddenly, came face to face with Bredin. He said in growing disbelief. 'You don't think this business at Walworth . . .'

'That poor bastard was knocked,' Bredin said.

'Murder?'

'That's it.'

'Impossible.'

Nally sat in thought, hardly a movement, where Bredin could see him. He could sense the awful impatience and anger: a packed charge that a few dragging moments of silence would ignite. It was important to know what Bredin knew. Down on the forecourt someone laughed, car doors slammed. There was silence.

Bredin drank back his liquor and as his great bulk tilted, Nally saw the butt of the pistol and its weight in Bredin's pocket.

Bredin? When had he ever aimed a pistol or why? It hardly mattered. There had always been battles and veterans, the savage elite, the rookies still in classrooms.

Bredin said, 'You know where Hennessy is.'

'I said I was looking for him,' Nally corrected.

'Where will you look?'

'Yes,' Nally said. 'Yes. We'll talk about that now. In a moment. You caught me unawares, winded me. I'm a little at sea.' Nally seemed to ask for patience, understanding: he circled the room, took spare keys for Feehan's car from the desk, left the Webley beneath a pillow in his bedroom, returned.

Bredin waited.

This would be the moment, Nally decided: a few words, a pattern of anxiety and then the query tossed in the midst of it, might work. 'Outlandish, hardly possible, is it? A murder at Walworth. This driver fellow you mentioned.'

'Hennessy.'

'Narking for a policeman somewhere, you said?'

'Yes.'

'Someone told you?'

'Cleary, at lunchtime. Terrified, the poor little bastard!' Bredin struggled for breath, against emotion. 'Now he's raw meat, half beaten to death for his trouble.'

'What policeman? Where?'

'Who in Christ knows!'

'And Cleary?'

'Down there, the hospital.' Bredin stood.

'My God!' Nally said in subdued outrage. But the plan was intact, a tight rope severed, curving, cracking like a whiplash but, strangely, falling limp and untangled.

'I want Hennessy,' Bredin said.

'Give me a minute, two minutes!' Nally said with a simulation of anger and confusion. 'Let me think.' He handed the whiskey bottle to Bredin . . .

Cleary, running or covering, had given things a twist, sent Bredin in pursuit of Hennessy, and suddenly everything was simplified. But Nally thought for a moment of the savagery of Feehan, of the danger there, the madness.

'A clever little fellow, isn't he? Cleary? Intelligent?' Nally said. 'I'm sorry.'

Bredin made a groaning noise, rammed fist against palm with

a thump of restiveness. A huge worn gnarled hand, Nally saw, blunted with years.

'Hennessy has a tart somewhere, I'm told,' Nally said suddenly. 'Rings her most evenings. A call box in Holloway.' He paused. 'We might be lucky, that's all.'

Bredin nodded, poured whiskey and drank it.

'When?'

Nally studied the time. 'Oh, nearly an hour yet.'

'The hospital,' Bredin said.

'Of course, the hospital.'

'I'll lead the way,' Bredin said.

'On this occasion we travel together.' Nally deferred very sincerely. 'Your car, you drive.' He patted Bredin's great animal shoulder, put on a leather driving jacket, a tweed cap. Helena read Nally's face in the foyer and wore a veil of compassion.

From the compound Nally could see the tall red-brick spires and Victorian turrets of the hospital across on Highgate Hill and, down far below and beyond, the vast sea of lights to the rim of the world. Freezing hard now but the snow, even pinhead motes, had cleared. Fireworks were beginning to explode, near and distantly, in the clear air.

Bredin's car smelt of vomit and grease and oil and machinery; the glove compartment was a litter of forgotten debris; the seats might be dirty. A strange day coming to a close, Nally thought, as they pulled away.

'He was beaten, you say?'

'Yes.'

'Badly?'

'Yes.'

Bredin, even on the icy road was pushing the throttle. When he had closed his door Nally had heard the thud as the gun struck it.

'This Hennessy? A mad dog, dangerous?' he said with a display of anxiety now. 'We should throw him to the Law, shouldn't we?'

'When I'm finished,' Bredin said.

Nally added little flares of kindling to the fire. 'And this dead navvy at Walworth, no head just pulp, I imagine.'

'Kirwan. A heading-driver.'

'Feehan savaged too, remember. Very badly, I'm told.'

'So you told me. I didn't know.'

Or didn't care, Nally could see. The steering wheel seemed to rest on the great protuberance of Bredin's belly and his hands dragged at it like a flier fighting for altitude.

'The company's car, of course.'

Bredin nodded.

'And now our little friend, Cleary.'

They turned left towards Archway roundabout and midway down the hill Bredin pulled across the oncoming traffic, held the car steady as a rock in the slip of dirt and salted slush, and parked it feet from the entrance.

The casualty hallway was a strange conservatory, an ugliness of geometry tacked on to the down-at-heel elegance of Victorian brickwork.

Nally looked beyond the grimy glass at arrivals, departures, traffic on the hill; he smelt and tasted the heat of the air, heard the clang of lift gates, touched the rubber sheet of a waiting trolley: the last frantic arpeggio of the senses for how many each day? He watched Bredin come from the desk with a fat man's splayed walk and Olympian shoulders.

Nally followed him.

At the casualty entrance a nurse said to Bredin, 'Are you a close relative?'

'Yes.'

'Not very good news, I'm afraid.'

'He's alive?'

'Very bad injuries, internal rupture, loss of blood ...' she recited. 'It isn't very pleasant, you understand? Do you want to see him?'

'I found him,' Bredin said.

She nodded and pushed open the door to the great sweep of beds, screened and unscreened, and the quiet speed of people and equipment. She pointed to a distant corner by a lift exit.

A bad location: Nally was looking and thinking.

She told Bredin, 'You should hurry, I think,' and he was already moving. She looked at Nally: a kindly man, she thought.

'I'm just a friend,' Nally said. 'And I won't intrude at a time like this.'

She nodded at his wisdom; a little compassionate smile. 'You can get tea at reception,' she said and hurried away.

Nally looked for a moment through the glass port of the door, could see Bredin marching on, listened to the clang of telephones, the hum from a lift shaft, thought of Hennessy, the phone box in Holloway. An hour would peel away like a skin, leave a new picture exposed . . .

Bredin's eyes were fixed on his target, the bright floral screen, the metal rails and runners. He saw nothing else: the beds, tired sleeping faces, and ghostly jaded sentinels were outside his tunnel of vision. As he watched, two young men, hardly more than schoolboys, scruffy as schoolboys, tired faces, white coats open, stethoscopes in pockets, emerged from behind Cleary's screen, approached and moved past him. The hot air seemed to gather about Bredin: his palms were sweating, his scalp.

When he reached the bedside and saw Cleary he had to fight the swell of sickness that rose in his mouth. Cleary on a plastic sheet was almost naked, the little stunted frame battered and hacked, rambling maps of skin black over pools of entrapped blood; blood leaking from his buttocks too; his face in tatters of flesh and an eye sitting out from its socket, a glaring orb, sick and oily like something horrendous from a joke-shop. As he watched there was an eruption of breath or pulse, clawing hands, a shuddering. Then it was over. Blood poured from his mouth and he was still.

'Are you all right?' a little Malaysian nurse was asking him.

'Yes,' he said; his own illness seemed to have died with Cleary.

He felt calm, looked at faces and tubes and cylinders and bleeping heart-screens as he left.

Nally was waiting.

Bredin said, 'He's dead.' He looked at Nally's kind grieving eyes and nodded. 'Thank Christ, he's dead!'

'There was no hope, they told me,' Nally said. 'I left them my card. The funeral arrangements, cremation, all that, down to me of course.' He looked at Bredin again. 'My sympathy, deepest sympathy. You held him in high regard.'

Bredin nodded.

Nally led the way. 'There's a pub down the hill. We'll have a stiff drink and it'll be time to move for Holloway. As I said, we might be lucky.'

. . . They saw the bonfire from the distance, the crowd, the children, the galaxy of stars and squibs.

'Drive up and past it,' Nally said.

They could feel the heat as they circled, hear the howl of air rushing into the vacuum.

'There's the phone box,' Nally said. 'Drive down a little into the shade.'

After the City's busy day of hedge and hustle it was nodding, stretching its legs and, until morning when the armies marched from suburbia again, it would be a great stone monument with only a little traffic and sparse hurrying mourners in the cemetery. Hennessy crossed London Bridge – the Tower was floodlit; the River in full tide, still as a picture – and went through Cannon Street, pointing for Moorgate and Hoxton. 'I was worried for you,' he remembered; and 'I owe you. You've done a good job.' He felt uneasy. Cricklewood, so long ago it seemed, he remembered it too: the alleyway, the face kissing him with grinding passion, an instant switch-on, a charade for the copper. The cold eyes.

He was tired. The comfort of Feehan's car, the warm glow of dashboard, the gentle heat, tried to pull him away. Not a lot of minutes left now and it would be over. A hundred minutes, maybe? Hardly.

Bonfires blazed on the steppes of Hoxton. With a little dishonesty, he thought, you grew tolerant of everything: he looked at his hands, red and tough on the steering wheel, always a little unclean. But clean enough. Only if he looked he saw their unpleasantness. In warmth you remembered only how cold you could be, how filthy you might let your body grow. You weren't so bad. In a score of derelict basements about the jewelled city he could find dossers on beds of newsprint and packing, within arm's reach of excreta and deflated wrinkled sheaths. You shrugged and felt amusement or pity and dumped your load. Dossers, deadbeats. You were better than that.

He pushed on through De Beauvoir and Ball's Pond. Feehan's car, for services rendered, was shining, cared for, polished like some meritorious gong. He tried to think of Archway and the tricks ahead but Kirwan was everywhere, smeared on his hands, beside him with the smell of fag and whiskey, groaning in morning agony, in the bright beckoning lights of every boozer.

He stopped in Blackstock, bought a flask of whiskey and drank.

The Law at Walworth had been the tedious day-to-day ritual, unhurried, innocuous. 'He was pissed, wouldn't you say, Pat?'

'Could be.'

'Careless poor bastard, eh?'

'Yes.'

'Shouldn't have left a loaded skip over the hole, should he?'

'No.'

You covered your tracks, covered Feehan's and Nally's too, buried Kirwan's honesty with blood and bone deep in Walworth. Dragging hours, little bound catalogues of questions, pages, pages, painted mugs of tea.

'Go home, Pat. Park it up, blow your mind with booze for a couple of days.'

The warmth of whiskey was a great comforting fix. He drank again, finished half the flask. He was in Hornsey Lane now, edging for Archway, and caution returned. He made ready.

Like Nally, he parked a block away and came up shrouded out of the dark frozen streets. He had expected that Cleary would be at the bus stop. There was no one.

He waited, watched: moments of assessment. Had Cleary struck lucky, clocked the girl and gone trotting in her wake to Holloway? She was too clever for that. Had there ever been a Cleary? . . .

He passed the Greek restaurant and Kirwan was with him again. And Maisie and how he might find her. What he would find? He crossed the slush and climbed the steps, let himself noiselessly into the hallway. The house was in darkness, a stirring in the basement. He stood for a long minute and listened. Not a sound only the distant television from below.

He took the stairs quickly, without pause, to the top landing. Kirwan's room. He pushed open the door. The scattered rubbish in the gloom should have been the moment of relief: Nally had come and gone and a deal was a deal. It was over, a battle won. But there was no elation. He went next door to his own room and packed, left not a trace of himself, not even a tattered paperback. He drank the half-flask of whiskey and packed the empty bottle.

He went downstairs to Maisie's door, rapped lightly, pushed. It was open. Time was running out. He peered into the strange limbo.

Maisie had drunk from Kirwan's bottle and stood watch against sleep like an exhausted sentry, in panicky dread of it, as if in the bizarre memorial room she had prepared for herself she were surrounded by ghosts. No one had come to see her in the study of her grief. She had thought in outrage that it might have excited neither comment nor attention if she had sat gay in the blazing lights of Cricklewood and sent music into the smoke since the moment of disaster. She was shocked by the insignificance of tragedy.

Sleep had needed only a momentary pause of her mind; and when it came she slumped helplessly in her chair, as if she had been dropped there, legs askew, and might never move again.

Hennessy heard the sound of her breathing as he paused in the doorway and stood in the almost total darkness. The candle of the dead was a pool of wax on the mantelpiece, a glimmer of light, and then for an instant it spurted flares of brilliance about the room. He saw Maisie in her wedding coat, her head tucked against the wing of the chair so that the straw boater, fruit-laden, sat out on a brink of yellow curls and covered her forehead. She would have wept at her own savage ugliness.

He went softly past her to the sugar-plum bed and groped for the parcel of banknotes, packed them in his suitcase. Almost over. He peered about at the dim faddy trappings of the room to take the memory with him without harshness or ridicule: the bric-à-brac of her entire travels was on the mantelpiece, presents from Margate to the Lizard. He saw the engagement ring on her finger. The candle flared again and drowned suddenly in its own grease and he inched for the doorway. A bedside clock suddenly spluttered a fragment or two of alarm and was still. Like Maisie, he needed a long deathlike sleep to heal him.

He went out into the evening, down the dark street to the car. He flung the suitcase on the floor by the passenger seat and lay back in weariness.

Guy Fawkes evening was coming to life. Kirwan might be drunk in the sky, he thought, with explosions of fire and colour, instants of mad laughter and then blackness and cataclysms of blinding happiness again. He might be thundering across the evening with peace finally in his grasp. A rocket burst like spray of an incoming tide and scattered across the heavens. Hennessy thought he heard the rush and thump of sea and the hoarse frothing drag on shell-paved canyons ... Kirwan.

When it was time he drove down to Liverpool Road and crept deep into the shadows of lower Holloway, a grimy congeries annealed in transience and dispassion. The bonfire was a towering beacon now; he could see the crowd, teenagers, children; fireworks crackled and showered moments of brilliance; on a fence post a catherine wheel raced into absurdity and blinding colour. He parked in the narrow street by the phone box and paused. The time was right, the phone box empty. He made the motions of dialling and searched the crowd for the emergence of her face ...

Nally had watched him arrive: the silver grey Mercedes at the phone box, the glare of the bonfire making a barrier more dense than darkness for Hennessy.

'He's here,' Nally said. He put a restraining hand on Bredin. 'I go first. When I'm at the car he's all yours. Be careful, of course.'

In the shadows, beyond fireglow, Nally skirted the target and when he reached the car he saw, first, the suitcase; then Bredin's lunging progress on the pavements. As Bredin pulled open the door of the box Nally sat in the driving seat. He had spare keys but the engine was running for the take-off. He saw the gun for an instant and the jerks of Bredin's shoulder were the shots, three, perhaps four, and Bredin was off, carrying his great weight before him, throwing his legs up and apart, lying back from the heat; and then the slapping bitterness of the evening.

Nally moved away. Hennessy's body had slid down until it seemed to squat on the floor; his legs pushed open the door and splayed and were still. Like a drunk, Nally thought.

As he drove past deserted houses, through the blowing heat of the fire, a roman candle flared and he saw in a blind window the glint of a metal fastener. Denim, he thought; and there was little surprise. She had come not to watch the demise of Hennessy, but to watch Nally. He didn't mind being studied.

At Highgate Nally showered again, drank brandy and was distanced from the grot and grime of it all.

Helena had laid out clothes for him and he dressed: a deep blue mohair suit, very fine, elegant; a shirt of palest cream and a bow tie with a wink of raciness that was just perfect.

Hennessy's suitcase was on his bed, open, the notes showing where Nally had broken the wrapping. He closed it, locked it in his wardrobe and decided.

He rang McLeod.

'The girl?'

'No trace.'

'Clever.'

'Very.'

McLeod sensed a trace of dissatisfaction. He asked, 'Is everything all right?'

'Not entirely,' Nally told him.

'Should I tidy up at Paddington tonight?'

'Oh yes. He'll be there. Very dangerous. A gun. One of ours.'

'I see.'

'Our driver and the little clerk. We won't be seeing them again.'

161

'Ah,' McLeod said.

'But the parcel's gone. The other half.'

'Well . . .' McLeod said with only a trace of concern.

'Buried, passed on, maybe?' Nally thought about it. 'We'll never know, I suppose.'

'But we're clear?'

'Oh yes!'

'Half a loaf,' McLeod said.

Nally paused and agreed. 'Yes, you're right, of course.' He heard Helena singing her little tune in the hallway. 'I'll be in touch tomorrow. A long story.'

'Fine,' McLeod said.

Nally turned off the fire, arranged his jacket and tie, took stock of the room and listened for the heavy drop of the bolts as he pulled his door.